THE BAKER AND THE BARRISTER

VANESSA GRAY BARTAL

DRY CREEK PRESS

CHAPTER 1

NCAA Final Four cakes were big business. Paley Marshall was glad, not only for the busyness that made her workday go quickly, but for the connection the cakes gave her to the sporting world. If not for writing the names of the remaining teams over and over on various cake designs, she would have no idea who played in the big game.

Her feet hurt, her hand cramped, but the smile never left her face. She was one of those rare individuals who loved her job. On the occasional day when all the cakes ran together and she felt melancholy, she only needed to picture the face of a child as she saw her birthday princess cake for the first time. Perhaps it was corny, but Paley believed all the extra love and attention she put into each cake somehow filtered to each recipient.

"You're not going to believe this one," her friend, Carla, called. Her back was to Paley as she sat at the computer scrolling through orders. Everything was automated now. The cakes came frozen from the store's warehouse. The frosting was premade in giant bags. The only non-computerized parts of the process were spreading the frosting, piping, and writing an inscription. Paley fully believed the moment the store could find a robot to do that, she and her crew would be out of a job.

"What is it?" Paley asked as she put the finishing touches on the last basketball cake. She was amazed by the odd things she had seen and the bizarre things people chose to have written on cakes. Sometimes they were so personal they made Paley blush and wonder about the state of humanity.

"Here." Carla handed her the printed order, shaking her head. "Men are pigs."

"What makes you think it came from a man?" Paley asked. They didn't read who the order was for until the cake was finished and it was time to print the price sticker.

"Read it," Carla urged.

"I want a divorce," Paley read out loud. "That's horrible."

"That's why it could only be from a man," Carla said.

"I hope this is a joke," Paley said. She pushed the buttons on the color machine to make the proper mixture of blue. Not much was left to chance anymore. It was a brave, new world for bakers. The blue mix squirted into her frosting bowl. She set it to mix, doing some squats while she waited.

"Don't tell me you're dieting again," Carla said.

"No, but I heard people who fidget burn more calories. I'm attempting to add movement into my everyday life." The frosting finished. She began the arduous process of slathering the cake, once again hoping it was a joke. Sometimes the funny cakes made her day, and Carla's, too. Last week she decorated one that said, "I'm sorry my pet mosquito gave you malaria." Not only was it funny, but it had been a real challenge to fit so many letters on a quarter sheet cake. For most of her coworkers, the job was exactly that—a job. They showed up, put in their hours, and went home. And that was okay; it wasn't as if they were recreating the Taj Mahal. But Paley put her all into the silly little job, going so far as to research and perfect writing techniques in her spare time. Right now she wrote in a modified calligraphy, something with an antiquated feel that was still easy to read. No doubt about it, she really loved her job.

Despite the hateful words, the cake turned out well. The icing was robin's egg blue, the writing white. It was pretty enough to be a China pattern, though Paley thought it resembled a Tiffany box. She boxed the cake and asked Carla for the ticket. Sometimes they took turns with their tasks, but generally Paley stuck to cakes and Carla the bureaucracy and customer service. They split the cleaning.

"All right, who is this going to? Hopefully someone with a good sense of humor," Paley said.

The printer whirred as the ticket printed. Carla tore along the dotted perforation, peeled the sticker and froze, staring, mouth agape.

"Carla, everything okay?" Paley said. Surely the cake wouldn't belong to someone they knew. It was a big city, after all. "That sticker is going to lose its sticky, and then you'll have to print another." A naturally efficient person, Carla hated having to redo anything.

"It's Aaron."

Paley looked around with a smile, expecting to see her husband standing at the counter. "Where?"

"Here."

Paley turned back around to see Carla fanning the sticker back and forth. "What?" The smile was still there, waiting for the joke, not realizing she was about to be the punch line.

"Paley, this cake was ordered by Aaron."

"There are lots of Aaron Marshalls in the world," Paley said. She tore the sticker from Carla's fingers to make her own inspection. Her husband's name jumped out at her. She scanned down to the address and phone number portion of the ticket, saw her own too-familiar digits, and froze.

"Is it some special occasion I don't know about? Some prank he's pulling?" Carla gently probed.

All she could manage was a shake of her head. Words were gone, as was the feeling in her fingers and toes. The sticker fluttered listlessly to the table, sticky side down so it stuck immediately to the stainless steel counter. Carla began picking at it, relieved to have something to do.

"I'm sure it's a mistake," she muttered as her fingernail scraped the last vestiges of the sticker. Scrape, scrape, scrape. The sound grated, pulling on Paley's overwrought nerves. She shook her head again. It wasn't a mistake. Somehow she knew that much. All the space between her and Aaron from the last two years came rushing back at her. She had blamed it on his law school; she had been wrong. He hadn't been busy with work. He had been busying himself to get away from her, and now he wanted a divorce.

The next shift streamed in, laughing and talking as if Paley's world hadn't imploded, as if her husband hadn't humiliated her in the worst possible way at her place of work. "Don't say anything," she whispered to Carla.

Carla shook her head. She was good for her word, but gossip this juicy would surely leak. Someone somewhere would check the cake log and know. Paley had a day or two at the most before her mortification became fodder for the masses. She bundled up the cake and tucked it under her arm, making her escape before she would be forced to converse with anyone. Her coworkers would find this odd; she was friendly, and they had a good working relationship. She couldn't care about it today, though. She had to see Aaron, had to clear up the mistake.

She tossed the cake onto the passenger seat and started the car, belatedly remembering to buckle her safety belt. Two miles from home, the car started to shudder and shake, warning lights came on, and smoke poured from under the hood. She made it to the end of the driveway before it gave out completely, chugging to a stop inches from the road. On a normal day, the death of her car would have distressed Paley. Today it didn't make the list of things that fazed her. She gathered the hateful cake and went to the front door where she faced a new surprise; her key no longer worked.

She rang the bell, holding the wretched cake to her chest like a shield. Aaron answered the door and crossed his arms, blocking access.

"Your cake is ready," Paley said, for lack of something else. She tried to shove the cake at him, but he refused.

"You can keep it," he said. His tone lacked rancor, but neither was it warm. It was bland and impersonal, exactly like their marriage.

"How could you tell me like this, Aaron?" she asked. "Why didn't you give me any warning? Why didn't you tell me in person?"

"Warning? Paley, I've done everything but engrave it on a letter. You can't tell me you think our marriage has been a success."

"You've been busy with law school," she said. "You work long hours."

"And you live in your own little world of unicorns and rainbows. I don't know what it's like there, but I would love to visit sometime," he said, some bitterness leaking into his tone.

"You're divorcing me because I'm cheerful and a dreamer?" she asked.

"No, it's because we're too different now, we're different people who want different things. You're happy with your cakes and your books and your garden."

"What's wrong with any of those things?"

"Nothing, but they're not me. I want more; I want better."

"We can work this out. We haven't even tried."

"That's because we've barely spoken in months," he said. "We have separate lives already. I'm making it official."

"I don't want to make it official. I don't want a divorce. I want to work things out," she said.

"I don't."

"How can you let this go without even trying to save it?" she asked. "Three years of marriage, two years of dating, and you're willing to toss it away without a backward glance?"

His eyes slid to the right of her face and he faltered, possibly for the first time in years. "There's someone else."

"Oh." It was one of those crisis moments every woman dreads, and Paley had no time to think of what she was about to say. All she knew was that her marriage was worth fighting for, and she didn't want it to end, even if it meant she had to forgive the utmost betrayal. "I still want to try to reconcile." The words hurt, but she meant them. She had taken her marriage vows seriously and only planned to say them once in her life, even if it meant she had to overcome a mountain of hurt.

"She's pregnant. As soon as the divorce is final, we're getting married."

"Oh." The cake felt like it weighed a thousand pounds. She dropped it and pushed it to the side with her toe. "I need to get my things."

"I sent your things to your mother's house," Aaron said.

"You're not going to let me in my house, to let me say goodbye?"

"Goodbye to what, Paley? You didn't want this house, you didn't want these things. You wanted to stay in our cheap little rental with the secondhand furniture. That was your house. This is mine. I already filed, and that gives me the advantage. A friend is handling the proceedings, and he's good. Don't make this worse than it has to be."

The worst part wasn't that he was right; the worst part was that she didn't even want to argue. She was decimated, an empty shell, a husk of the person she had been this morning. She turned. He closed the door. She saw her car and rang the bell again. He jerked it open with an impatient frown.

"What is it now?"

"My car is dead," she said.

He sighed at the imposition she presented, as if she were a Girl Scout with an order form who wouldn't take no for an answer. "Fine, I'll take you to your mom's." But you're on your own from there, was an unspoken guarantee.

CHAPTER 2

The ride to Paley's mother's house was awkward, to say the least.

"I brought five thousand dollars into the marriage," she said, making one attempt at a plea for justice.

"We spent that much and then some trying to keep your jalopy going. The house and my car are in my name," he said.

She sighed, a heavy sound that did nothing to ease the anxiety in her chest. What was she going to do? Aaron must have been wondering the same thing.

"You need to get a new job, Paley."

"I like my job," she said.

"You have a college degree and you decorate cakes for a living. Maybe it's time to grow up," he said.

"Maybe I'll take advice from you when you stop impregnating other women," she said. He shot her a look of surprise. Sarcasm wasn't usually a weapon in her arsenal. She was passive by nature, and not even passive-aggressive. All she wanted from life was peace and happiness. She thought she had found that with Aaron.

They had been so happy their first year of marriage. They rented a tiny cottage with a grand garden; it had resembled a house in a fairy tale. They relied on Paley's tiny salary while Aaron went to law school full time. He had worked hard, becoming second in his class. The prestige of that led to an offer from one of the big law firms in town, and that was when things went downhill, at least in Paley's mind. With the promise of a six-figure salary in his future, Aaron hadn't been content in their tiny rental, he hadn't been content with his used Honda. He had wanted the McMansion and the Lexus, pronto.

"'Give them to me now,'" she sang the song from the old Willy Wonka movie. Aaron shot her a look of disgust. He hated it when she burst into song. He must hate everything about her, and she somehow hadn't realized. When had that happened? Was it when she uncharacteristically put her foot down and tried to get him to wait for the house and car?

We owe so much on your school loans, she had cautioned. Why don't we stay in this house until that debt is paid off and then we can upgrade? We'll be in better shape financially. Based on his reaction to that statement, one would have guessed she had suggested blowing up a baby hospital. Aaron had gone ballistic. He railed at her for days over all the ways she held him back, regardless of the fact it was she who had supported them for the last three years of law school and she who did all the work around the house, including a hundred percent of the cleaning, cooking, laundry, and yard work.

"I even ironed your clothes," she muttered. And she had done it cheerfully, thinking it was what a good wife did. Some might say she had deferred her dreams and career for him, but they would be wrong. She had enjoyed helping him succeed, had enjoyed working at the store and puttering in her garden. She had been happy, blissfully so, and all the while her husband had been building a life with someone else.

They reached her mother's house. She put her hand on the door and Aaron spoke. "Look, if you agree to a dissolution, we don't have to go to court."

"What's in it for me?" Paley asked, taking a page from his book.

"You won't have to try to afford a lawyer, and you won't have to try and find one who can match mine."

She wasn't fooled; the dissolution would work in his favor, but she didn't care. She had no fight in her. She never had. "I'll need money to survive for a while." This morning they had been partners. Now she made the request shamefully, like a beggar.

"I guess I could try to find a couple thousand for you."

Two thousand dollars, that was what she was worth to him, what five years of her life meant to him. She had labored every day to support him, to feed him, to clothe him, and all that work amounted to two thousand dollars. Briefly she wondered about the next Mrs. Marshall. Would she take care of him the same way? Or would they have to hire a maid? If so, she was bound to charge more than two thousand dollars. "Sounds good," she said. She eased from the car and let herself into her parents' home. Unlike the first door she had tried that day, this one opened immediately.

She followed her nose to the kitchen where her mother had made a feast fit for a twenty people. She glanced up at Paley with a smile, "Oh, hey, hon." Her parents were from northern Wisconsin and had never lost their twang. They could still be counted on to routinely pop out phrases such as, "You betcha," and "Don'tcha know." The fact that her mother had prepared so much food was a testament to the fact she already knew about the separation. Alternately feeding or ignoring problems was her parents' solution to everything.

"Hi, Mom." She slid onto an oak bar stool. Her mother's kitchen was all oak and powder blue, as if the 80's had stopped by for a visit and decided to stay. Stranger still, her mother had remodeled it no more than a year ago, ripping out the sleek lines and modern design that came with the house.

"Supper will be ready in no time at all. Do you want a snack?"

"No, thanks. I'm not hungry. Where's Dad?"

"Oh, he's watering the lawn or some such. Tis the season, you know."

Her father had a love affair with green grass and was willing to use any amount of chemicals to make it that way, cancer concerns notwithstanding. No one was allowed to walk on the grass. His wife wasn't allowed to stake bird feeders or decorations that might harm the grass. He was obsessive about trying to get the right blend of seed, water, fertilizer, and weed killer, not realizing by taking things to such extremes, he often killed his lawn so it was dotted with crusty yellow patches and scorched earth. The ugly patches drove him to try harder and use more product so he spent a good six months of the year babying his dead yard. He was a lesson in all the ways retirement could be brutal without a solid plan. One year Paley and her siblings pooled their money and hired a lawn service for him. He spent the entire time watching the workers with narrowed, suspicious eyes, sure they were sabotaging his hard work. After they were done, he retrieved his supplies and undid everything they had done to try and fix the lawn. And then he blamed them when the grass came back browner and crisper than ever.

"Listen, Mom, I know Aaron had my things delivered here today. You must be wondering about that."

"Just a little hiccup. I'm sure you two will work it out," her mother said, pointedly ignoring eye contact as she made a roux for the gravy.

"I don't think we will, Mom."

"Nonsense. Every couple has hard times. You need to get in there and work on it until it's better."

No amount of work would undo the baby he was having with another woman. "Mom..."

"Taste this." Her mother shoved a fork of pot roast between her lips. It wasn't the first time her mother had stifled any attempt to talk about her problems, and it wouldn't be the last. If Aaron thought she lived in a dream world, she had nothing on her mother.

"Really good," Paley said. "Do you need any help?"

"No, thank you. You go watch TV or something."

"I guess maybe I should unpack."

"No." Her mother smacked a potholder on the counter for emphasis. "There will be no unpacking. Unpacking spells defeat. You hear me, Paley? You unpack, and you won't work on things. This is temporary."

That was where they agreed. Paley needed to find somewhere else to live, as soon as possible. She loved her parents, but their brand of crazy rubbed off too easily. One month of living at home and she would be sporting an apron and a beehive in a vain attempt to woo Aaron back.

"Maybe I'll say hi to Dad." She stepped outside and didn't see her father anywhere. Maybe he was in the garage. She took a step and he spoke.

"Off the grass."

There was no way to get to the detached garage without walking through the grass. Perhaps there was a method to his madness after all. Defeated, she went back inside and down the hall to what would be her room. Her mother had put her in the tiniest guest room, no doubt to urge her to go back to Aaron as soon as possible, as if lack of space could induce her to resume life with a man who had cheated on her. It probably could, Paley admitted to herself. If not for the fact that Aaron didn't want her, she probably would be willing to turn a blind eye and go back. She had inherited too much of her parents' preference for ignoring things. If not for the other woman and her impending baby, Paley could probably return to her marriage and pick up as if nothing out of the ordinary had happened, facing her daily routine with a smile and chipper attitude. But that wasn't going to happen because Aaron didn't want her. Now what?

She scanned the tiny room as if it could offer clues or advice. Her boxes towered and teetered, blocking her view of the mirror. That was probably a good thing. She had no desire to stare at the sad specimen her reflection would show—twenty six, fifteen pounds overweight, and about to be divorced. Where was her happily ever after? She remained staring listlessly at the boxes until her mother called her for supper.

Her father smelled overpoweringly of weed killer, making it hard to eat or breathe. She choked down enough food to satisfy her mother, offered to help clean up, and retreated to the safety of the den when the offer was refused. The lack of conversation over supper had been as draining as if they had talked of nothing but the separation.

Her parents' attempts to ignore the situation at all costs was going to cost Paley dearly.

She meandered over to her mother's movie collection, trailing her finger absently over the titles. For as long as Paley could remember, she had been fed a steady diet of Disney cartoons and musicals. They stared back at her now, mocking, confirming all the ways her life had gone off track. Her Prince Charming had turned out to be a toad. She didn't fool herself she had been perfect in her marriage and all the problems were Aaron's fault, but at least she hadn't strayed. At least she had been willing to stay and work things out.

Bypassing her mother's collection, she moved on to her father's. His movies contained a different sort of fairy tale, action flicks and spy thrillers where the strong hero always caught the bad guy and came out on top. Tonight his brand of oblivion appealed to her much more than the romance in her mother's collection. She selected the first of the Bourne trilogy and popped it in the DVD player. No Blu-ray here—it was miraculous her parents weren't still watching VHS. They had only reluctantly upgraded after Paley and her siblings bought them a player for Christmas.

The movie droned and Paley watched with half-hearted interest. She had seen it before and knew the outcome, but it provided a distraction from her thoughts. When it was over, she went to bed, hoping her mental exhaustion would equal sleep.

After spending an hour searching the boxes for her toiletries, she was physically exhausted as well. Aaron had packed her toothbrush and even her toothpaste, leaving no detail to chance so that she might have to return to the house to retrieve something. He had packed her clothes, her books, her movies, and even her favorite pots, pans, and utensils. The sum total of her life fit into twelve boxes, and she took some comfort in the order. If only her emotions were so easy to organize and file.

She went to bed and fell almost immediately asleep, too quickly to be relieved by her body's easy acquiescence. The blissful deep of unconsciousness didn't last long, however. With a start, she woke two hours later. Her arms were reaching to the spot beside her. For Aaron? Not likely. When was the last time they slept a full night in the same bed together? She had tacked his late hours and odd disappearances up to law school. How many of those nights had been spent in the arms of his mistress? Her mind cast about for a distraction, something, anything other than the picture of her husband and the other woman.

The Bourne movie popped into her head and put itself on replay. Paley tried to replicate it scene by scene and was frustrated when she couldn't. She had just watched it. Even though her attention had been half-hearted, how could she not remember? When it became clear sleep was becoming a distant memory, she slipped out of bed and back to the den. The movie was still in the player. She turned it on and watched again, this time with full focus.

In many ways, her life was like Jason Bourne's, Paley thought as her hand lay listlessly inside a bag of half-eaten potato chips. On the television, Jason was currently roundhouse kicking six bad guys, conveniently flashing a view of his solid twelve pack. So maybe they weren't identical twins. But they had both woken up to a new and unwelcome reality. They both had no idea who they were. They had both been wronged by someone. Wouldn't it be wonderful if she, like Jason, could take control of her life and fix everything that was bad? The movie ended and she put in the second in the series. When that was done, she watched the third until her parents were awake and it was time for breakfast.

The movies had comforted her in a way she couldn't explain. As she stood in the shower and analyzed why, she realized it was because the princess movies relied on someone else for a happy ending. In each movie, the heroine had been rescued by a handsome prince. Not so Jason Bourne. He rescued himself, and he hadn't let anyone stop him from reaching his goal. He had been prepared for every situation, capable of handling what life threw at him, even when what life threw at him was certain death.

After breakfast her parents left to do whatever it was they did.

Paley had no idea. It was her day off, and she was sad about that. How was she supposed to fill the long lonely hours? She had intended to work in the garden at her house, to try and bestow charm and originality to the McMansion that looked like every other house in the neighborhood. Now the day stretched out before her as one long attempt at avoiding her thoughts.

She meandered back to the den and perused her father's movie selection again. She could rewatch the Bourne movies, but that left too much opportunity for her mind to wander. Instead she reached for James Bond. She had never watched a Bond movie before. Her father owned them all. He had thoughtfully placed them in chronological order for her. She started with Moore and was halfway through Connery when her parents arrived home.

They traded worried glances when she stumbled zombie-like to the kitchen but didn't stop her when she grabbed her food and took it back to the den.

She watched James Bond all through the day and long into the night before finally falling into a restless sleep. As with Jason Bourne, she found Bond oddly comforting. He always knew what to do, always did the right thing, always took care of business.

The next morning was work. Paley had barely slept in two days, but she wasn't tired. Instead she was numb. She plastered on her usual smile, hoped it would be convincing, and set to work.

A short time later the store's manager, Herb, interrupted her. Somehow he looked like a Herb, even though she had never known another. His hair was slicked back with what she hoped was gel. He sported a thick mustache and left one too many buttons on his shirt undone. If he had driven a Camaro, the picture of a '70's lothario would have been complete, but he drove a conservative Japanese sedan. Even though he had been her boss for three years, she'd had very little to do with him in that time. She preferred to fly under the radar, to show up every day, do her job well, and go home again. No muss, no fuss, that was her philosophy. They said hello to each other whenever they happened to meet. Two years ago, he promoted her to the head of the department, and that was the extent of their interaction.

Today she guessed he had heard the rumors and wanted to make sure she was okay. While a part of her was touched at his concern, she felt embarrassed by the pending intrusion into her personal life. She need not have worried, though. Herb had no concerns about her or her life.

"I'm promoting Trudy to department head," he declared when she had barely taken a seat across from his desk.

"What? Why? Did I do something wrong?" She mentally surveyed her work, checking for holes. She found none. She had done a good job at the bakery, excellent really.

"No, I think she's a better fit."

She stared at him, sure he was joking. "Trudy thinks a lot is one word."

"Isn't it?" he asked, and he was serious.

"Last week she did an engagement cake and wrote 'Tom an Vera.'"

"So?"

"It's and, Herb, Tom and Vera."

"So she saved a letter and used less frosting. That's the kind of resourcefulness we need in these hard financial times."

"She can't spell. Don't you think grammatical correctness is sort of important when you're writing words all day?"

"You can oversee her and help her out."

"You want me to oversee the woman you're promoting to my job?" she clarified.

"We're all on the same team, Paley. Oh, but this shift will result in a reduction of your pay. You're going to need to pick up some extra hours."

Not for the first time Paley wished she were one of those people who knew how to stand up for herself. She was a doormat, and everyone knew it. She stared at Herb, unable to muster one word in her defense. What would Jason Bourne do? No, nix that. People who crossed Jason Bourne usually ended up dead. She didn't want Herb dead. Did she? No. Probably not. She shook her head. Definitely not.

She wanted her old job back with no fanfare or confrontation. Instead she stifled everything she felt and went back to work, as Herb probably knew she would. For the first time she wished her store was part of a union, but that was probably a cop out. Why should she expect a union to fight for her rights when she wasn't willing to?

Trudy stood at the counter, a triumphant smile on her overly made-up face. "Back to work, Paley," she said and immediately left to take her fourth smoke break of the morning.

"What happened?" Carla whispered.

"Herb gave Trudy my job. I've been demoted." The words hurt. After Aaron, all she had was her job. It wasn't much, but she loved it.

"What?" Carla hissed. "Trudy is literally the worst employee in the department. You know why he did this, don't you?"

"No," Paley said. She had run out of understanding for people. All she wanted was to keep her head down and get by in life. Why lately did it seem like everyone was intent on keeping her from it?

"Because he thinks he has a shot with her," Carla said.

"But they're both married," Paley said.

"Trudy's been going after him pretty hard. Maybe it was to get your job, or maybe that's who she is."

Herb walked by them, presumably on his way to join Trudy outside. He eyed Carla and Paley suspiciously. They moved apart and returned to work, but Paley couldn't shake her lingering disillusionment. What was wrong with people? She wanted to believe the best of everyone, wanted to believe there were good people in the world. Until a few days ago, she had succeeded nicely in being an optimist. But now everything was upside down. The world was a dark, unfriendly place, especially for a gentle soul.

The day turned busy. Paley was thankful for the steady stream of work. She lost herself in the beauty of the flowing script she put on each cake.

"That's wrong." She hadn't heard Trudy approach, but now she hovered over her shoulder, staring at the cake she had just finished. Paley picked up the ticket and double-checked the order.

"You're the best. That's right," she said.

"It's your, y-o-u-r," Trudy said.

"No, it's y-o-u apostrophe r-e, as in 'you are.' It's a contraction."

Trudy looked at her in confusion. "Now you're saying there's a dash in there?"

"No, not a dash. This." She showed her the apostrophe and explained the contraction again. Trudy stubbornly shook her head.

"It's your. Fix it."

"It's not wrong," Paley said. There were many things she could tolerate; grammatical errors weren't one.

"Fix it or you're fired," Trudy said.

"You can't fire me," Paley said.

Trudy practically rubbed her hands together in expectant glee. "Maybe not, but I know someone who can. Maybe I'll have a word with Herb about your insubordination."

You're is a mystery to her, but insubordination she knows, Paley thought. Was it worth it? Was the fight over proper spelling worth her only source of income? Could she reasonably handle getting divorced, living with her parents AND being unemployed right now?

She scraped off You're and rewrote it as Your, ignoring all her better instincts. What choice did she have? She needed the job. It was one thing to have principles and another to need money to pay the bills.

Trudy walked away, a self-satisfied smile on her face. What had Paley ever done to her? She had been a kind and fair supervisor. What had she done to earn such vitriol? She felt as if she had woken up, had her sleep mask ripped off, and now viewed a different world. Things had changed somehow, and she couldn't understand them. Last week she had been a happily married woman with a job she loved. Now she was soon to be divorced, living with her parents, and borrowing their car to get to a job she now hated. Worse, the future stretched before her in an endless line of repeats. Tomorrow would be like today, and the next day would be the same, and the day after that. Where once her monotonous routine had seemed safe, it now felt stifling. How could she stand it? But what could she do to change it?

Nothing. She had no money to start over and wouldn't know what to do anyway. She wasn't adventurous enough to step out on a ledge and try something new. She would go on decorating cakes until her hands became too arthritic to hold the pastry bag. Then she would enjoy a meager retirement and die alone in a state-run nursing home.

Such was Paley's mood that the death part of the equation sounded like a welcome friend.

CHAPTER 3

"Oh, hey, hon," was her mother's familiar greeting when she arrived home. Her accent was in full force, which meant she had something further to say. "Someone called for you today."

"For me?" Paley said. Her world had become small; it consisted of Aaron and her friends from work. She couldn't imagine who would be calling for her.

"You betcha. I left her name and number on the table." Not taking any chances, she scurried to the table and handed Paley the message.

"Acacia Billings," Paley read before setting the note back onto the table.

"Aren't you going to call her back?"

"No."

"Why not?"

Paley shrugged. There was no way to explain the complete inertia that had taken over her existence, the inexhaustible nothingness that now inhabited inside her. She didn't want to do, didn't want to feel, didn't want to be. It took as much energy as she possessed to simply wake up and keep going, to keep putting one foot in front of the other day after day after day. And when she thought about all the days that stretched out ahead of her in an endless barrage of nothing, she could barely lift her arms from her body, let alone her feet.

"Honey, about the car…" her mother began tentatively.

Paley sighed. "I know, Mom. I know. I need to get my car fixed so I can stop using yours, but it's going to be an expensive repair, and I don't have the money." Especially because today she was demoted and now making even less.

"Can't you ask Aaron…" her mom began, but Paley cut her off.

"No, I can't ask Aaron. I can't ask him for anything," Paley said tiredly.

"He's your husband," her mother said.

"Not for much longer."

Her mother huffed in frustration, and Paley looked up, startled. "Paley, you haven't done anything to try and mend fences."

"There's nothing to do," Paley said.

"How do you know if you don't try?" her mother asked.

"Mom, nothing I can possibly do will make his girlfriend un-pregnant," Paley said.

Her mother's mouth rounded in a little "O" of surprise. Paley stood and headed for the back door. It was as if the soil called to her, physically pulling her in its direction, promising hope and healing, if only she could get her hands in the dirt. She opened the door, one foot dangling out.

"Off the grass," her father called from somewhere unseen like one of those recordings at the airport that reminds people not to leave bags unattended.

Sighing, Paley drew her leg back inside, went to her room, and collapsed onto the bed. Sleep was a welcome friend lately, and she slid into it with ease. Sometime later her mother's voice echoed down the hall, calling her to supper. Yawning, she stumbled down the hall and sat at the table. She wasn't especially hungry, but she didn't have to be. Food was an anesthetic and always had been. Her nose smelled chocolate. She scanned the counter and saw a tray of brownies behind her mother's head. Brownies were the equivalent of her mother's atomic bomb, a recipe so good, so decadently perfect she only pulled it out when she needed to relay something serious. Paley tensed, not certain if her mother had attempted to relay heavy-duty comfort or something more sinister.

They ate in silence. Paley stuffed bites of beef, gravy, and mashed potatoes between her lips while her eyes darted between her parents.

"So," her mother said at last. The heavy northern American accent was so thick it made it sound as if there were a hidden U somewhere in the word, drawing it out to make it a statement all its own.

"So," Paley replied. Unlike her parents, she had been raised mostly in Maryland, giving her no accent that made the word anything more than one syllable with a long O.

"It would seem some things need to happen here," her mother said. She reached behind her to the tray of brownies and began to dole them, sliding a hefty one onto a plate and setting it before Paley. Her father watched jealously, abashed the first piece hadn't gone to him like normal. It amazed Paley the two of them could have been married for three decades and yet her father remained clueless to his wife's ways. He had no idea of the undercurrents taking place in his kitchen. All he knew was that brownies were being bandied about and he didn't yet have one.

"What, Mom? What needs to happen? Because I really don't know." Paley sniffled. Her mother pushed her plate closer. Paley dutifully picked up the fork and took a bite, the sweet, heady brownie mixing unpleasantly with the salty taste of her tears.

"Let's look at the practicalities. You need to get your car fixed."

"I have two thousand dollars to my name," Paley said.

"I wouldn't think it would be more than that," her mother said, squinting questioningly at her still-oblivious husband who was now happily eating a brownie. "If it's more than that, your father and I will help. I know you like working at the bakery, but you need to get a better job, something that pays more with benefits."

"Easier said than done," Paley muttered.

"You need to get back out there on your own," her mother added, more gently this time.

Paley's head snapped up. "You're kicking me out."

Her mother shook her head. "Sometimes baby birds need a nudge."

"I haven't been in the nest for a lot of years," Paley said.

"No, but I can see you settling back in here, almost like the marriage never happened. You're hurting, and we hurt with you." Her gaze darted to her husband who was now scraping his plate, apparently not even listening to the conversation. "But you have to keep going, to keep doing. You can't hide in the basement and watch action movies all the time."

The dam on Paley's emotional reservoir was about to break. She was going to lose it, big time. Their family wasn't into big, dramatic, emotional scenes. They were soldiers, the kind who did their duty without chatter or complaint. It was the gist of what her mother was telling her, to get back on the horse, to keep on keeping on. But all Paley wanted to do was sleep and cry and sleep and cry some more. When the phone rang, she lunged for it, if only as a distraction from the coming turmoil.

"Hello," she said, fighting hard against the press of tears.

"Hi, may I speak with Paley Marshall, please?"

"This is Paley," she croaked.

"Hello, Paley, this is Acacia Billings. I'm positive you don't remember me, but we met several months ago at a mixer my firm offered for prospective law students. You arrived with your husband, Aaron."

"Yes," Paley gasped, her chest spasming with pain at the mention of her husband's name. She cleared her throat. "I remember you. You're a legal secretary for, um, one of the big names I can't recall." She did recall that Aaron had salivated over the possibility of working for the firm.

"Piedmont Bonvoy," Acacia supplied. "I remember you brought cookies to the mixer."

Paley winced. She wasn't supposed to have brought food, but in her family bringing food was an absolute. Aaron had been livid when she presented the tray of cookies at the fancy, catered event.

"Yes, sorry about that," Paley said, her face flushing from the memory. Was that why their marriage hadn't worked, because Aaron saw her as some kind of unsophisticated rube, too crass and undignified for the life he desired?

"Oh, goodness, sweetheart, please don't apologize. Those were the best cookies I've ever eaten. I've been dreaming of them since that night."

"You…you have?" Paley said uncertainly.

"Yes, that's the entire reason I tracked you down and, let me tell you, it wasn't easy."

"Oh. I'll make you some more, if you like," Paley offered.

"Could you make a thousand of them?"

"Uh," Paley stammered.

"We're having another function, and those cookies would be the perfect topper for the event, decorated in the style of our choosing, of course."

"When would you need them?" Paley asked.

"Next Saturday night."

Paley mentally calculated her budget. She could probably afford fifty bucks to buy ingredients. "Okay, sure. Would you like me to bring them to your office?"

"We haven't discussed a price yet," Acacia said.

"A price for what?" Paley asked. She tensed. Was the woman planning to charge her?

"A price for your cookies. A bit of online research assured me fifteen hundred dollars is the going rate."

"Wait, you want to pay me?" Paley asked.

Acacia chuckled again. "Were you going to do it for free?"

"Yes," Paley admitted.

Acacia clucked her tongue. "Don't do that again, honey. This is business. You're going to spend money on the raw materials and time to make them."

"Okay, sorry," Paley said, feeling flustered.

"Do you need an advance for the ingredients?" Acacia asked.

"No, I can cover it."

"Very well. I'll have your check ready on Friday when you drop off the cookies," Acacia said. "Give me your email address and I'll send you a picture of what we want."

"Okay, thank you." Paley gave her address, disconnected, and turned to survey her parents.

"What was that about?" her mother asked.

"I'm making a thousand cut out cookies for a party," Paley said.

Her mother beamed. "See? Good things are happening already."

Paley nodded, not sure a thousand cookies would be enough to make up for a cheating husband and his forthcoming baby, but at least it was a start.

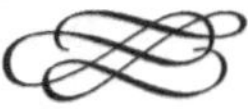

CHAPTER 4

Paley learned a lot that week, namely that she was woefully unprepared to bake and decorate a thousand cut out cookies.

To start out with, she took her car to the shop. It was going to be fifteen hundred dollars, everything she would make from the sale of the cookies. But at least it hadn't cut into the two thousand dollars that now amounted to her life's savings.

Next she began looking at the logistics of a thousand cookies. Quantifying recipes was a tricky business. Her normal cookie recipe made two dozen. If she multiplied it enough to make a thousand, it would likely destroy the integrity of the recipe and be a big mess. She felt comfortable doubling it because she had done that before, but that would still only give her four dozen cookies when she needed eighty four dozen. And she had to do it all in her mother's small kitchen, in her mother's small oven.

"Hey, I know. The church," her mother said on the first day.

"You want to go pray I'll actually be able to do this?" Paley guessed.

"No, the church has a commercial kitchen that sits empty unless someone is using it for a wedding or funeral. Let's call and see if it's open. We could do this there."

"Mom, that's brilliant," Paley said, already reaching for her phone.

The church had been available and Paley and her mother lugged all their supplies there. In addition to having the increased space they needed, they also had extra baking sheets, saving Paley the hassle of having to wait for her cookies to cool before she could load up another tray. The first day she made three hundred cookies, with the help of her mother.

The next two days were spent the same, minus her mother. Within four days, Paley baked and froze twelve hundred cookies, leaving herself with plenty leftover, in case she broke some or messed them up.

On the fifth day, she made mass quantities of frosting and practiced piping until she had the design perfect. Thursday and Friday were spent frosting. And frosting. And frosting. On Thursday she frosted for fifteen hours, until late into the night when the church was dark and deserted. Paley packed her boxes carefully and loaded them into her car. She would finish the final few hundred cookies at her parents' house, and then she would have to drive into the city to deliver them.

She arrived at the venue a half hour earlier than the designated time. Acacia met her there, check in hand. Paley had been prepared to unload all the cookies herself, but an entire crew of workers met her at the door and carried the boxes. Acacia opened a box and inspected them.

"Perfect, Paley, so perfect. Thank you. We might call on you again sometime. Do you by chance have any cards, in case someone asks and wants to hire you?"

"Um, no, but I could scrawl my number on some napkins for you," Paley said, smiling so Acacia would know it was a joke. It was the kind of statement that would make Aaron furious, as if he thought she would really scratch her name on a napkin and hand it to a high-powered lawyer.

Acacia laughed. "If worse comes to worse, that's what we'll do."

"Thank you so much for thinking of me," Paley said. "I hope the cookies are a hit."

"I'm sure they will be."

It was time for Paley to go, but she paused, saying a mental goodbye to the cookies.

"Was there something else?" Acacia asked.

"No, I was…I was saying goodbye to the cookies. We spent a lot of quality time together this week. It feels a bit like leaving my baby for all-day preschool the first time, except people are going to be biting my babies' heads off and devouring them," Paley said, and Acacia laughed again.

"You're too cute," Acacia said, swiping beneath her eyes.

I am? Paley wondered. When was the last time anyone called her cute? It filled up a little bit of her crumbling heart, even if it was coming from a middle-aged secretary she would likely never see again. "Thank you. Have a nice party."

Acacia nodded, smiling, and gave Paley a little wave before turning her attention back to the task at hand. *That's that,* Paley thought. It had been a fun project, a pleasant distraction from her troubles. But it was over and, despite what Acacia said, unlikely to be repeated. People didn't actually taste a cookie at a party and want to hire the baker for more. Did they?

Yes, as it turned out. Paley got three calls for cookies and one asking if she did birthday cakes. "Absolutely," she remarked. Cakes were actually more of her specialty than cookies, seeing as how it was what she did for a living, if the paltry amount she made at the grocery store could be called such.

She made an additional five hundred dollars. Flush with cash now, she blamed herself for what happened next.

"Why'd you put that there?" Trudy hovered over Paley's shoulder, inspecting her work as she did every day.

"What?" Paley asked, inspecting the cake. She thought it looked good, perfect, in fact.

"That comma." Trudy pointed.

"That's not a comma, it's an apostrophe," Paley reminded her. "See the word is it's, it's a contraction for it is." The request had been for a cake that said, "It's Friday!"

Trudy shook her head. "That's not right."

"Yes, it is. If you say it without the comma, it's wrong."

"That don't look right. Take it off."

"No," Paley said, and the bakery came to a stand still as everyone looked at the two women.

"I'm your boss, and I say take it off," Trudy said, her tone filled with a gleeful sort of authority.

"I'm someone who has a degree in English literature, and I say no. This is how it's written. The apostrophe stays," Paley said.

While still holding eye contact, Trudy reached out and scraped off the apostrophe with her bare hand. Paley mashed down on that hand, pushing it all the way to the bottom of the cake. Trudy shrieked. "What are you doing?"

"Making sure you got it all," Paley said.

"You're fired," Trudy said, withdrawing her hand and flinging bits of cake and icing all over the place.

"You can't fire me," Paley said.

"We'll see about that," Trudy said and stormed away.

In the end, Paley was fired. Whatever little rebellious spark had lit in her had wanted to quit, to rail against Herb and Trudy and tell them all the many, many ways they were wrong. The more rational portion of her, the one now terrifyingly close to poverty and homelessness, bit her tongue and thought warmly of the unemployment benefits she could now collect.

Thanks to her recent baking ventures, she had three thousand dollars to her name and a functioning car. And that was all—no health insurance, no house, no job, and no prospects. She planned to go home and hibernate in the basement, despite her mother's protests. She certainly had no plans to answer the phone, but then she saw Acacia's name and leapt for it.

"Hello, Paley, this is Acacia."

"Hi, Acacia, how are you?"

"I'm well, how are you?"

"I'm..." the worst I've ever been, literally minutes from being homeless, destitute, and divorced. "Well."

"I have a bit of an awkward question for you, and I want you to know in no way will you hurt my feelings if you're not interested in what I'm about to propose."

Paley wriggled in her seat, thinking whatever Acacia was about to say sounded more interesting than the reality of Paley's life. "Yes?"

"Do you cook things other than cookies and cake?"

"Yes, I can cook anything," Paley said.

Acacia let out a little breath, as if this were a relief. "Are you good at cleaning?"

"Yes."

"My boss is looking for a housekeeper. I know this is probably a long shot, but you were the first name that came to mind, at least temporarily until I can find somebody else."

"A housekeeper?" Paley repeated. "Like a maid?"

"It's a bit more than that. Yes, there would be cleaning and laundry involved, but also cooking. He works long, crazy hours. Basically he needs a version of me, but at home. Someone to make sure he's being looked after. It's a live-in position normally, but I know you're married so…"

Paley interrupted her. "I'm not, actually. Not anymore."

Acacia paused. "Oh, I'm sorry."

"Thank you, but please continue about the job. I'd like to know more about it so I can give it my full consideration." She glanced at the interior of her car, still parked in the grocery lot. The shabby sedan represented all she now owned in life, and suddenly Acacia offered her a way out, a hand up, not only a job but a place to live, at least until she found something better. No matter the next words out of Acacia's mouth, Paley would take the job. Even if she said the guy spent his free time dressing like a clown and hunting humans for sport, it was likely a better option than her current reality.

"Piedmont is…he's sweet, don't get me wrong. In that way, he's a nice boss. He never yells or makes crazy demands. But he's also a genius who lives in his own head most of the time. He needs someone to sort of float peripherally around him and pick up the slack, to anticipate his needs before he realizes he has them."

"Sounds like a wife," Paley noted.

"Yes, that's exactly it, minus any romance. He's not…he recently suffered a terrible heartache, and he's not up for dating right now. But he needs someone to be there to make things work when I'm not around. To be honest, if I'd known you and your husband weren't together, I wouldn't have asked. You're young and pretty, and I don't want it to be like…" she trailed off, not knowing what to say.

"Let me assure you romance is the very farthest thing from my mind right now, both men and lawyers," Paley said. If Acacia heard the hard edge to her tone, Paley hoped she realized it was directed at Aaron and not her. "I need a place to regroup, to lick my wounds and figure out what's next. This sounds so ideal I feel like an angel beam should be filtering through the phone, from your head to my ears. I can definitely cook and clean, and I'll try my best to do the other stuff, to settle his life without being intrusive or obvious about it."

Acacia let out a little breath that sounded like a sigh of relief. "Excellent. Your face popped to mind when we learned his last house-keeper quit, and I hoped…Anyway, can you stop by tomorrow? I'll give you a key and go over everything with you."

"That sounds excellent. Thank you so much," Paley said. She was in the parking lot of the place she'd been fired from, and yet she felt a bit of hope and release, as if maybe things were beginning to look up, at least a little.

CHAPTER 5

The next day Paley met with Acacia to receive the lowdown on her new job. By that night, she had loaded her boxes into her car and unloaded them again in a posh Georgetown brownstone.

Her quarters would be in a converted attic, and Paley was so excited she could barely contain her enthusiasm. She had always liked hidden spaces, quiet cubbies, out of the way alcoves. To know she was now going to be living in one was more exciting than she could believe. She didn't even care that she had to ascend three flights of stairs to get there. She dashed up and down them repeatedly, carrying boxes and bags until her legs felt like they might fall off. After that, she explored the house.

Acacia had told her the guy was out of town for a couple of days, so it was the perfect time to settle in and have a look around. She did so unabashedly, disregarding her usual reserve. She would be washing and sorting this man's underwear; it was better for both of them if she learned where they went and how he liked to have them arranged. Therefore she left no stone unturned in her search, taking note of the precise arrangement of his bedroom spaces. Were things color coordinated because that was the way he liked them or because it was the way the former housekeeper had preferred them? Either way, Paley had no plan to disturb the arrangement.

To her relief, she found no hidden nightmares, no drugs, no basement room filled with chains or anything else of that nature. In fact the basement was filled with a highbrow gym and entertainment center. Paley's stomach pooch jiggled, reminding her she needed to hit the gym and work off the fifteen pounds she'd gained since marrying Aaron. He had never mentioned her excess weight. She thought it was because he didn't mind. Now she realized it was because he didn't care enough to mind.

Pushing away thoughts of Aaron, she took stock of the fridge and pantry, then made a plan for upcoming meals and a list for the grocery. Acacia had given her a credit card belonging to her new employer. At the end of the month, Paley was to turn in all receipts to his accountant, along with receipts for any money she spent on his behalf out of pocket.

"Is there a budget?" Paley had asked. "A limit?"

Acacia had shrugged. "Reasonable."

Paley hid her frown. One woman's reasonable was another man's cheap. Aaron had been forever chafing at her imposed budgetary restrictions, often calling her a Quaker or Amish for her frugality. Paley had felt like sticking to a monthly budget was merely a responsible thing to do, especially when they were paying for law school. She sighed a little as she closed the refrigerator door. At least she was no longer on the hook for her husband's massive school loans. That was one relief in the midst of so much heartache.

With her belongings unpacked and the house explored (and still clean from its last cleaning, whenever that was), Paley changed clothes, went downstairs to the gym, and worked out. Sweating felt good. Not as good as eating, but that was how she had wound up in her current condition in the first place. She worked out for a solid hour, until sweat poured off her, and then she showered in her new bathroom, climbed into her new bed with a book, and eventually drifted to sleep.

The next morning she learned how to use the fancy coffee

machine. It took a few tries and some hints from the internet until she got it right, but the end result was worth it. The coffee was by far the best she'd ever had. Cup in hand, she meandered to the back yard and sat down, enjoying the quiet of the morning. The yard was good sized for being in the city, and it was fenced. And that was the best she could say about it. It was well manicured, but too sterile for her tastes. Her imagination took over as she stared at it, mentally planting perennials and annuals. It could be spectacular, in the right hands. Not hers because she was temporary, but someday some garden loving someone might take possession and turn it around.

When her coffee was finished, she went inside and decided to bake something. Acacia had hinted that, though her new employer usually ate healthy and worked out, he also occasionally liked to indulge in a treat, especially at breakfast. Paley found a recipe and made muffins that were loaded with carrots, raisins, and nuts. Because she wanted them to be fresh and warm, she set the batter in the fridge in order to bake them in the morning.

With nothing left to do for the rest of the day, she changed her clothes and worked out again, another hour. After that she took a long bath and read while she soaked. She hadn't taken a bath in forever. Aaron hated it when she did, for reasons Paley had never been able to fathom. He'd said it was because she "stewed in her own filth," but Paley thought it was merely one more fundamental difference between them. He was the type of man who liked to grab a quick no-nonsense shower first thing in the morning and she was the type of woman who liked to languish in a tub of warm water late at night. She had never begrudged him his morning shower; why had he felt the need to comment on every bath? And why had she let it deter her from taking them? Somewhere along the way she had started giving up little pieces of herself, trying hard to conform to what he wanted her to be. In the end, it hadn't mattered; he had still shoved her aside for something he felt was better.

Paley went to bed early and fell asleep quickly, not stirring when the front door opened and her new boss arrived home.

Acacia had warned her he would probably do so, so Paley woke early, at dawn. The hour was unusual for her, but she tried not to show it, hastily throwing on clothes and brushing her hair and teeth before going to start the coffee.

He wakes at four, works out for an hour, showers, then eats breakfast and coffee before leaving for work, Acacia had told her.

Every day? Paley had asked. Aaron had been disciplined, but not that disciplined.

Every day, Acacia had said, nodding.

So now Paley was up before five, racing to bake muffins and make coffee. She had just taken the muffins out of the oven when a man walked into the kitchen and stopped short. Paley did the same and quickly set down the hot tin of muffins. He was young, much younger than she'd been prepared for.

"Did you break in here to bake, or are you my new housekeeper?" he asked, tilting his head at her in question.

"Maybe both things," she said, and he laughed in surprise.

"They smell good." He perched on a high stool. Paley poured him a coffee, taking note of how he took it, cream but no sugar. Then she plated a muffin and slid it in front of him, busying herself with plating the rest of the hot muffins.

"Thank you," he said. He took a bite, closed his eyes, and made a little "mmm," sound. When his eyes opened, he realized she was staring at him and fought a blush. "Sorry. So good."

"Thank you."

"Can I ask your name? It's possible I'm supposed to know and I forgot. It's a thing with me, sort of scatterbrained to the point of it being a disability." He tapped his temple.

"We've met seven times," she said, a little bit irritable.

He pressed his lips together, looking chagrined. "Sorry."

She smiled and shook her head. "We've never met, sorry. I have no idea why I'm giving you a hard time when I'm supposed to be conciliatory." She wiped her hand and held it out to him to shake. "Paley Marshall."

"Piedmont Bonvoy," he said, shaking her hand in return. "And please don't be conciliatory, please be yourself."

"Okay," she said, giving him a little curtsy.

He laughed.

"What? I curtsy to everyone. It was my senior superlative in high school. 'Most likely to have knee replacement from constant curtsying.'" What was she saying? Why was she babbling this way to a stranger, and an employer, no less? She had no idea except something about his kind face put her at ease. He seemed like the kind of guy she might have been friends with in high school.

"I think it's time you had a new superlative—most unusual housekeeper I've ever had. Also best baker." He held his last bite of muffin aloft before downing it.

"I'm sorry, really. I have no idea why I'm babbling this way. It must be a pre-dawn thing. After the sun comes up, I am totally normal. Ish."

"Nah, I like it. All the deference and normalcy get a little tiresome. I can honestly say I've never laughed at one of my housekeepers before. Except one who fell down the stairs, but she ended up with a broken ankle, and I felt like a total heel for laughing."

Paley snickered at the mental image and pressed a hand over her mouth. "Sorry, I laugh when people get hurt."

"Me, too. It's a real problem for a trial lawyer who makes a living from wrongful injury lawsuits. I giggle all day long in court," he said, and Paley laughed again.

"I know you get this all the time, but you're really young to be a lawyer. I thought Acacia was kidding about you being a genius. I guess not."

"I could show you my MENSA card, if you like," he offered.

"Really? Sure," Paley said, perking up in interest.

He frowned. "No, that was a joke. I don't actually have a MENSA card and, even if I did, I wouldn't carry it around like some kind of weirdo."

Now she frowned. "Without the card as proof, how am I to believe you're an actual genius?"

"The card could be faked; how could you believe its veracity?"

"That's a good point. I'm going to need some other standard proof of genius from now on," she said.

"Does the fact that I graduated law school before I was old enough to legally drink buy me any leeway?" he asked.

"No. Any idiot can go to law school," she said, thinking of Aaron.

"This is the toughest interview from a housekeeper I've ever had. But what about you? You look awfully young to be a housekeeper. All the other ones have been old. How do I know you actually are one?" he said, resting his weight on his elbows as he leaned forward.

"I'm also a genius, but I chose not to go to law school. So I guess I'm sort of a cautionary tale of what you might have become, if law didn't work out for you," she said. "Use my life as a lesson. Tell the others."

He laughed again and tilted his head, the other direction now. "I'm genuinely not sure what to make of you."

She gave a little shrug, self-conscious now. Stop babbling, moron. "Can you tell me any food preferences you might have or anything else you think I should know about the care and keeping of your house?"

"I like all food, I try to be health conscious with the occasional treat thrown in, and most nights I don't get home until after eight. I'll most likely eat supper then, although sometimes I eat out. I'll never remember to call, so sorry in advance. I might eat here every night or I might not."

"Let me ask you a difficult question." She rested her hands on the table.

He tensed. "Go ahead."

"Do you prefer I leave your meal warm, with the possibility it could get dried out, or would you prefer me to leave it in the fridge and let you warm it on your own?"

He rubbed his temples. "Asking the hard questions on the first day; I was so not prepared for this. I suppose in the fridge and I'll do the hard work of pressing the microwave buttons myself."

"If you find it's too much for you, call me, and I'll come press the microwave buttons for you. Or if Acacia calls me, I can make sure to have it ready for you."

"See, now I'm not sure if you're odd and cuttingly sarcastic or normal and kind of helpfully sweet," he said.

"Time will tell," she said, refilling his coffee without being asked. "Another muffin?"

For a moment he looked like he was going to say no, and then he slid his plate to her with a meek nod of his head.

CHAPTER 6

The house still didn't need cleaned. Paley checked Piedmont's room and made his bed. She sniffed the sheets to make sure they were fresh. They were. She gathered his dirty clothes and wiped down his bathroom, tucking a few things away he'd left out. *He's kind of a slob*, she thought. Was it because he had a hired person to pick up for him, or was it because his genius brain didn't tend toward things like tidiness and organization? All the smartest people she'd ever known had also been a bit scattered. What he'd said about being bad with names made her think the culprit was his high intellect more than laziness or indulgence. The brain only had so much available space. When it was taken up with intelligence, things like common sense tended to fly out the window.

She finished and made another cup of coffee, feeling restless and overpaid. Bonvoy paid her ten thousand more than she made at her last job, and that didn't even include the perk of room and board. She would have to buy health insurance but, even so, she would make more than enough to live on, and even a hefty surplus amount for savings, barring any sort of emergency. She was doing basically everything she had done as a housewife—cleaning, cooking, shopping, and laundry—but without the added burden of working another job outside the home. She couldn't help but feel a bit guilty about that.

With nothing else to do, she took her coffee and meandered outside, her mind once again filled with possibilities. It could be spectacular, a true oasis. Maybe she should use some of her money to plant a few things. That could be a way to fill the empty hours and ease her guilt over making too much money with so little to do. But maybe he wouldn't like that. Maybe he liked things plain and dull and void of character. Seeing as how she'd had exactly one surface conversation with him, she had no idea. Her phone beeped with a text. She picked it up and read the message with a smile. She hadn't talked to her high school best friend, Mattie, in years, much, much too long. Judging by the tone of the message, they were going to pick up like no time had passed between them.

Your mom told me you got dumped. Sad trombone.

Nice, Mr. Sensitive. I'm heartbroken and destroyed here, she replied.

That'll teach you to listen to me. Guy was a putz. You should never have married him.

You said that about every guy I dated, she reminded him.

Not true, I never said it about me, he replied.

You should have, she said.

Ha, ha. See, I cry to cover my weeping. At least now we're free to elope. How's Friday?

No good, I'm still married and started a new job.

**audible sigh* Fine. I'll wait until you're legal.*

You say that to all the girls. Hopefully.

Ha, statutory jokes are awesome. Let's do dinner ASAP. How's Friday?

Don't you have a date? she asked.

You, hopefully, he replied.

Her hand hovered over the phone. Aaron hadn't liked Mattie, and the feeling had been mutual. Paley's friendship with him had seemingly petered and died. She believed it was the natural course of things when one became married, but now she regretted the loss. Mattie had always been a wonderful friend to her, loyal, supportive, and fun. With the loss of Aaron, she could resume their once-close friendship with zero guilt. *Friday is perfect.* She hit send and stared into the backyard some more, wondering and hoping that things would be as easy and fun with her former friend in real life as they were in text.

M eanwhile at work, Piedmont Bonvoy hadn't given his new housekeeper another thought, but that was his nature. He tended to focus obsessively on things that were in front of him, his mind so busy with information it had to make a concerted effort to zero in on the important things. Most of the time, that was his job. Not until lunch arrived did he summon the memory of the early morning encounter with Paley Marshall. He stared at the lunch she had handed him, amused. No housekeeper had ever packed him a lunch before. He should probably tell her he bought lunch every day, but he hadn't had the heart after she handed him the tidy little brown sack as if she were the mom and he were the kid heading off to school.

Out of curiosity, he opened the sack and stuck his head inside. When it was too dark to see what was inside, he withdrew the items one by one and made his inspection. She'd cut an apple into wedges and secured it together with a rubber band. There was a sandwich, and it looked good. So good, in fact, he took a bite without really thinking about it and then paused in his inspection, staring at the sandwich. It was good, really, really good. So good he took it apart and looked at it curiously. What made it so good? He had no idea, so he put it back together and continued eating it.

After devouring the sandwich and the apple, he moved on to the crackers and cheese, plus an assortment of nuts and dried cranberries. They were all the things he liked, and it was a lunch he would have prepared for himself, if he ever packed a lunch for himself, which he never did.

He pressed the intercom button. "Acacia, could you…"

She poked her head in the door. "You rang?"

"Yes." He cleared up the remnants of his lunch and stuffed them in the trash. "I met my new housekeeper."

"Paley," she reminded him.

"I know," he said, though not unkindly. He sometimes had trouble with names—Acacia was good with names and more often than not had to remind him. "Where'd you find her?"

"She made the cookies for the party a couple of weeks ago," Acacia said.

"The purple ones? The ones I ate three of?" he asked.

"I didn't keep count of how many you ate, but, yes, those," Acacia said.

"How did she progress from caterer to housekeeper?" he asked.

"I don't know. I had a feeling when I met her you two would hit it off."

He frowned. His secretary wasn't the sort to fix him up with a woman, but that sounded awfully like what she might be doing. Like usual, she read his mind.

"I thought she was married, when I asked," Acacia interjected.

"She's not?"

"In the midst of a divorce," Acacia replied. "And pretty heartbroken over it, from the sound of it. She didn't ping on my radar as being in search of love, is what I'm saying. I think you're safe there."

"Good," he said, relieved.

Acacia noted the crumbs on his desk. "Did you eat a packed lunch?"

"I did. I feel like I'm ten. And she handed me a travel mug of coffee on my way out the door, made exactly as I like it," Piedmont said. "This one might be a keeper."

Acacia nodded, a little bit stunned. Piedmont was friendly and affable, but he didn't normally warm up to strangers so quickly. She had worried, when she made the arrangement, that perhaps Paley would fall for Piedmont. Now she began to fear it might be the other way around. She would make some discreet inquiries on his behalf, to make certain Paley was as genuine as she seemed. Acacia usually had a good sense about people, and she liked Paley from the beginning, when she shyly presented a plate of cookies at the law school meet and greet several months ago. She had taken the cookies to be polite, because it wasn't the kind of thing one presented at an event like that. But after tasting the cookies, she had been a dedicated fan of the woman's talent. Even so, Piedmont had been through a lot the last few months, and Acacia was protective of him. She didn't want to see him get hurt again, even by a girl she liked.

CHAPTER 7

Paley and Piedmont settled into a happy little routine that suited them both. In the morning, she rose with him at dawn and prepared his coffee and breakfast. She baked something nearly every day, but, knowing he was health conscious, sneaked fruits and vegetables into the mix. A couple of weeks in, he finally brought it up.

"I think it's so nice you bake new things for me each day, but I don't usually eat so many treats," he said, his tone gentle in case he offended her.

"That muffin has kale in it," she said, sipping her coffee sedately as she gauged his reaction. He didn't disappoint. He pulled the muffin away from his mouth and studied it, his eyebrows upraised in surprise.

"Kale? In this?"

"The chocolate ones had beets and the granola clusters were made with quinoa. They've all been high protein and low carb," she said.

He blinked at her. "What about the raspberry Danish?"

"Do you think I'm psychotic? That was full butter. You don't mess with perfection. But that was the only splurge the last couple of weeks," she assured him.

"Did you make these recipes up?"

"No. I found them on a blog about how to fool your toddlers into eating healthy," she said.

"Not sure if I should be grateful or offended," he said, reaching for another muffin.

"Do you want to go back to how it was before, when you thought you were eating dense, rich treats every day with no idea I was sneaking in health food?"

"I demand it," he said.

"You're the boss," she replied, but it didn't feel like it. He was always so nice, ever polite and kind, seemingly not egotistical in any way. He was one of the bright young stars on the law scene. She'd heard Aaron speak about him in half adoring, half envious tones, never realizing they were the same age. Aaron was only now getting his career started; Piedmont was already on top, making high six figures, and would likely be invited to make partner within the year.

"On that note, you don't have to get up with me every day," he said. "The weekends especially, take some time off."

"I'm already awake, and my afternoons are fairly free. I have downtime. Unless this is your clever, polite way of saying you want your space and I'm crowding you. Because I have a coffee maker in my room, I could..." she trailed off, her gaze traveling to the stairs.

He reached out and touched his fingers lightly to her arm. "You're not crowding me. I'm not passive-aggressive about things. If I want space, I'll tell you. This was me trying to make sure you're taking time off."

"I think you're paying me too much," she blurted. Unfortunately she said it as he sipped coffee and he sputtered, pressing his fingers to his mouth.

"What?"

"You pay me too much."

"It's the same I've paid my last three housekeepers," he said.

"You paid them too much, too."

"It's the going rate," he assured her.

"It's too much. I have guilt. I have way too much free time, and my room and board are included, too." She sighed, glad to get it off her chest.

He laughed uncomfortably and swiped a hand over the back of his neck. "I have to tell you I negotiate multi billion dollar settlements and contracts for a living, and not once has anyone ever complained because they're paid too much."

"I'm not complaining; I'm being honest."

"You cook, you clean, you do the laundry, you run the errands and stock the household supplies, oversee scheduled maintenance. If I had to pay for each of those things individually, I'd likely end up paying more than I pay you."

"Yes, but I also live here. It's too much."

"It's not too much."

She opened her mouth, but he pressed his palm to it. She nodded instead. He shook his head.

"I'm paid to argue. Do you really think you can win?" he asked.

She nodded. He laughed and dropped his hand. "I've also been planting things," she blurted.

He froze. "Like pot?"

She grimaced. "No, not pot. What on earth?"

"I'm sorry, but you said it so cryptically."

"I didn't know if you'd mind, so I've been sneaking plants in like I'm bringing a shiv to prison and planting them one by one."

"Why?" he asked, but he sounded more curious than angry.

"Because gardening is kind of my thing, and you have an outdoor space begging to be made over. At first I thought I'd do it a little at a time in case you noticed and got mad, but I've never seen you go out there, so I figured I should fess up before it becomes a problem." She paused. "Is it a problem?"

"No. As you said, I never go out there. Occasionally I have people over and we use the deck. Otherwise, consider it your playground."

She beamed at him, and he smiled in reply. "Your lunch," she said, pressing the bag into his fingers, along with his travel mug.

"What is it today?" he asked.

"A surprise," she said.

He grinned. "It's ridiculous how much I look forward to opening the bag each day."

She checked the clock. They had ten minutes before he had to leave. "Can I ask you a question?"

He braced himself. She said it a lot and always followed it with something nonessential, but he always had the same reaction, as if preparing himself for something unpleasant. "Yes."

"The pay is good, but Acacia said I'm your fifth housekeeper. Why did the others quit?"

"I'm not the easiest person to work for."

She laughed. "Are you joking? You're the nicest boss I've ever had though, sorry, that's actually not saying much." She shuddered, thinking of creepy Herb from the grocery store.

"First I would submit to you we're in a sort of honeymoon phase here where everything is new. Second I would tell you I'm difficult in less obvious ways."

"Because you're a genius," she said, tapping her temple.

"Because I'm quirky and live in my head a lot and expect people to read my mind. I'm demanding about weird things and expect those around me to anticipate my needs. The last few housekeepers and I haven't clicked. I never felt comfortable with them, and they seemed perpetually frustrated with me because I was unable to articulate my wishes." He gave her a thoughtful stare. It had been different with her from the beginning. He wondered why that was.

"Acacia hinted at as much. She said you needed someone like her, but on the home front, someone to sort of hover in your atmosphere and try to arrange things and anticipate your needs."

"You seem to have a knack for that," he said.

"You're not the first genius I've known, actually. My friends at school were all brilliantly gifted. You remind me of them. You're all a different breed, a special kind of strange, but I like it." She paused. "Your friends were probably gifted, too."

He shrugged. "I didn't have friends. I was ahead of everyone academically but behind them in age. I didn't fit anywhere." He was friendly and outgoing, but he didn't connect with many people. He hadn't connected with anyone in recent memory until Amelia and then… He pushed the painful thoughts away, shaking his head.

"Have another muffin," Paley whispered. "For sadness." She opened his lunch sack and dumped the muffin inside.

Piedmont smiled. She was warm and kind and he liked her. Best of all, he never had the sense she was flirting with him, unlike a lot of women he encountered. Being considered a catch was something completely new. He grew up being the nerdy kid, the brain. The last few years he'd undergone the metamorphosis of his dreams, finally gaining muscle and growing into his looks. But that and the prestige of his job seemed to be all women cared about. Except Amelia who… He pushed the thoughts away again.

"I should go, but, oh, look at me, remembering to tell you far ahead of schedule I definitely won't be home for supper tonight. Please don't make anything for me," he said.

"Okay, thank you. That's actually a bit of a relief because I'm going out, and I was worried about leaving food set that long in the fridge."

He wondered, suddenly, where she was going and who she was going with. But they didn't have the kind of relationship where he could ask, nor even where he should be curious. She was his housekeeper. She was fun and friendly, but there was nothing more between them. "Have fun."

"You too," she said. "Take them to the cleaners today."

"Who?"

"Does it matter?" she asked.

"No, but rest assured I always do." He gave her a little salute with the hand not holding his lunch and let himself out the door.

CHAPTER 8

Paley met Mattie downtown. When she saw him across the room, she started to cry. He picked her up and spun her around, holding her tightly a minute before setting her down.

"I'm sorry," she said, sniffling and, using a proffered napkin, wiped her nose.

"For what?" he asked.

"For letting go of our friendship," she said.

"You were married, it was only natural."

"I should have married someone who could be friends with you, too, who would understand," she said.

"Of course you should have. I was trying to be nice." He grimaced. "Didn't suit."

"Not at all," she agreed, hugging him again. "I'm so ridiculously glad to see you."

"You, too," Mattie said, returning her hug. He had already put their names in. They were seated shortly and perused the menu before they started to talk. "So. What's new? Still decorating cakes?"

"No. Are you ready for this? I live in the posh section of George-town in a massive three story brownstone."

"Did you get that in the divorce?" he asked, agog.

"No, I haven't gotten anything in the divorce because we're not divorced yet. I got it on my own."

"Lottery? Drug mule? Insider trading?"

"All three combined. I used my insider information to play the lottery on my way home from making a drug delivery in Venezuela."

"Busy girl."

"You know me, always ambitious," she said, and he laughed.

"What's the catch, really?"

"I'm a housekeeper for a rich lawyer," she said.

"Like Downton Abby?" he asked.

"Exactly. When I'm there, I affect a British accent and everything. It's kind of exhausting, but you know me, I never complain."

"You complain incessantly, you miserable harpy," he said, reaching over to tweak the hair resting on her shoulder.

"Yes, but now I do it in a British accent, so it sounds really, really good," she said.

"Speaking of accents, I talked to your mom, don'tcha know," he said, imitating her mother's intonation.

"Did you go to their house?" she asked.

"And risk walking on the grass? Never," he said, and Paley's heart filled to the brim at being with someone who knew and loved her. She and Mattie had been friends seemingly forever. He'd seen her at her absolute worst, and he adored her anyway. And the same was true for him.

She took his hand and pressed it to her cheek. "Mattie, I love you so much."

"Are you getting soft on me, Anderson?" he asked.

"It's still Marshall, and no. I'm working you over to fleece you later," she said, letting go of his hand with a shove.

"That's my girl," he said. "See what you can take for me from the manor house while you're there."

"I have some dirt for you, but you'll have to dig it from beneath my nails," she said, holding her hands out. "It's not much, but a few million more trips and you'll have enough to pot a small flower."

He whistled appreciatively.

"Nothing's too good for my best friend," she said.

"No, I was whistling for backup. Time to truck you to the looney bin. Seriously, Paley, you're showing me your finger dirt. We've known each other too long."

"I scrub, but it doesn't come out, and it's kind of a badge," she said.

"The kind that says you need better soap?"

"The kind that says I planted things and nurtured life today."

"Are you also the gardener?"

"Unofficially," she said. "And happily." She beamed at him.

"That was creepy."

"Sorry, I'm a bit out of practice at smiling."

"That bad, huh?" he asked, resting his chin in his hand.

Paley let out a breath. She never would have complained to him if she and Aaron were still together. But now that it was over... "It was miserable. You want to know how miserable?"

"Yes, please," he said.

"I'm working for a guy who pays me to do everything in his house for him—cook, clean, wash and fold his underwear. And he's so ridiculously grateful. I mean, the guy's my boss and has every right to order me around, yet he's always so careful to tell me how much he appreciates the things I do for him. I did all the same things for Aaron for free while working another job, and yet he always found a reason to criticize. Nothing was ever good enough for him. The whites weren't white enough, the house wasn't clean enough or decorated well enough or fancy enough, the meals were too heavy, too bland, not enough something. And then there was me as a person."

"How could he possibly find fault with my Paley?"

She gazed up at him, tears pooling in her eyes. "He did. A lot. Everything was wrong. He made me feel stupid and ignorant and ostracized. I started eating to numb myself. I gained fifteen pounds, another strike against me. He made me feel like a fat, miserable failure, and the worst part is I let him." She swiped impatiently at her eyes. She hadn't realized how far she'd sunk with Aaron until she wasn't with him anymore.

"What a heartless loser," Mattie said, kissing her hand and giving it a squeeze.

"I'm sure if he were here, he could list some legitimate faults of mine for you. I am in my own little world most of the time," she said. "And I do…"

"I'm well acquainted with your faults, Paley. But guess what? I have faults, too. I still love you, and you still love me. It's what you do with the people in your life, you love them in spite not because. You don't try to make them perfect; you try to love them even though they're not."

"Wow, that's really good, Mattie," she said, brushing at her eyes again.

"I've got a million of them," he said, blowing on his nails and buffing them on his chest. "Come on, enough talk about the piece of trash who is, thankfully, no longer in your life. Tell me what else is going on with you now. Do you plan to stay at Downton forever?"

"I don't know." She sighed. "What is wrong with me, Mattie? Why can I never figure out what I want to do with my life? You've always known; I've never known. I always feel like someday some magic mirror is going to reveal to me what my true purpose is, but until that day I'm doomed to wander the earth forever, lost and looking."

"You know what your problem is, Paley? You were born out of time. If you were hatched fifty years ago, you'd be a housewife, and because you wouldn't know anything different, you'd be happy. But instead you were born now, and you're crazy smart, so you have society telling you that you should be driven and ambitious, preferably in some kind of STEM field. But in your heart, you're happy to cook and bake, to read and drink tea and putter in your garden."

"Mattie, what have I done without you in my life these last few years?"

"Been miserable and alone?" he guessed.

She nodded. They spent a long while talking about him, to Paley's relief. Not only did she not want to dwell on herself or her problems, she was deeply curious about what was going on with him. When the meal ended, they went to grab coffee, and when they could linger there no longer, Paley invited him back to the house to watch a movie.

"I don't want to brag, but I have a loveseat and television in my third floor maid's quarters," she said.

"Why did you have to tell me? Now I'm eaten away with envy and will have to score better maid accommodations of my own to outdo you," he said.

Piedmont wasn't home when Paley let them in. Vaguely, she wondered where he was and if he was on a date. He hadn't mentioned a girl, and she had never seen anyone but him at the house, but that didn't mean he wasn't seeing anyone. He was handsome, rich, and ambitious, a winning combination in competitive Washington DC.

"Wow," Mattie said, stopping short in the entryway to appreciate the lovely townhome. "This actually is really nice and enviable. Tell me something bad to tamp down my jealousy."

"I decorated my own divorce cake," she blurted and told him the story of Aaron's cake order.

"That was too much bad. Now I'm glad you have such nice maid quarters," Mattie said, tucking his arm around her shoulders on the long walk up the stairs. They sat on the loveseat and watched one of their mutually favorite movies from high school. By the end, Mattie was asleep. Paley touched his arm.

"Mattie, do you want to stay or go?"

He blinked sleepily at her. "Stay."

She slipped off his shoes and covered him with a blanket as he curled into a ball on the tiny loveseat. When he was set, Paley washed her face and crawled into bed.

Piedmont saw the strange car in his drive and wondered who it was, wondering if Paley was reconciling with her husband. He felt a moment of regret over the thought, and then selfish. Just because she was a good housekeeper and he was comfortable with her was no reason for him to want to keep her to himself. She was young and deserved to have a life outside his house. Still, the thought of her leaving, of breaking in someone new and adjusting to having someone else in his space, filled him with dread. The next morning as he was working out, the door alarm beeped, alerting him to the fact that Paley's mystery guest was likely going home.

When he saw her at breakfast, she greeted him with a smile. "Did I hear someone leave?" he asked.

"My best friend from high school stayed over," she explained.

He nodded, slightly relieved at the thought she'd apparently had some girl time. "How was your night?" she surprised him by asking.

"Boring," he said. It had been another function, one he'd shown up to alone. Which was worse, to try and score a date to these things or show up alone and feel like chum in the water for predatory women? He still hadn't figured that out.

"It's Saturday," she said, presenting him with fresh chocolate croissants. "Treat day."

"Saturday is quickly becoming my favorite day," he said, reaching for the pastry with maximum enthusiasm.

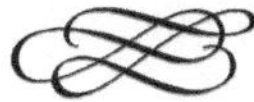

CHAPTER 9

Paley was happy. Perhaps happy was the wrong word; she was *content*. She had settled into a routine at her job, one that gave her plenty of free time and creative leeway. She cooked and baked interesting things for which her boss was always appreciative. She cleaned and did laundry, but doing so for one man was hardly a fulltime venture, especially when many of his things needed to be dry cleaned. In her many hours of free time she worked in the garden, which was taking shape and becoming something else entirely, something special with the potential to be spectacular in a couple of years when everything grew in. In her remaining free time she read and worked out, so often she had quickly shed ten pounds. To be so happy in the midst of personal turmoil was a pleasant and welcome surprise. By all rights she should be miserable. Her husband had cheated on her and kicked her to the curb, quite literally. A couple of months ago she had been heartbroken, destitute, and homeless. Now she had a home, a job, money in the bank. As for Aaron, that still hurt, and probably would for a long time. He'd left scars on her heart, not only with his infidelity but with the painful relationship they'd shared while married. Her trust in her own judgment was shaky. How could she have been so wrong about him? Or had she been right in the beginning but he somehow changed? She didn't know. It was one of the things she pondered while she worked out, running at a moderate pace on the fancy treadmill.

Piedmont's home gym was nicer than any professional gym she'd ever been to. He had a treadmill, elliptical, rowing machine, spin bike, climbing wall, and weights. Paley didn't know quite what to do with the climbing wall or weights, but she made good use of everything else. The rowing machine took her by surprise, mostly by how much she loved it. Unlike running or using the elliptical, it didn't require her to keep the focus on her body. She could sit and row while her mind wandered. It was ridiculously soothing, and she had worked herself up to a half hour of rowing a day.

She was almost finished with her run and about to switch to the rower when Piedmont suddenly appeared at the base of the stairs, blinking at her in surprise. Paley tripped, catching herself on the treadmill's bars as she pushed the emergency stop and came to an ungraceful end. "Sorry," she blurted.

"For what?" he asked, still blinking at her in astonishment.

She remembered, all of a sudden, that she was wearing a sports bra and spandex shorts, not the sort of attire she would ever wear in front of her boss, or anyone really. But she usually had the house to herself when she worked out.

"I don't know. It felt like I should be sorry about something."

"Don't be," he said. She could tell he was having trouble keeping his eyes on her face. They wanted to stray south to her extremely exposed midriff, but he wasn't the kind of guy who ogled women. The struggle was real. Paley put him out of his misery by reaching for her t-shirt and slipping it on.

"Sorry," she said again.

"Now what?"

"Being half naked in your basement," she said.

"Don't be," he said, giving her an exaggerated wink that made her laugh.

"Creeper alert," she said. "What are you doing home? I mean, not that you can't be home, it's your house. What I meant to say was how can I help you, sir?" She curtsied, and it was his turn to laugh.

"I took the afternoon off," he said.

"You…you what?" He hadn't had a day off in weeks, since she'd first arrived, minus the occasional Sunday.

"It happens occasionally," he said. "I heard the sound down here and thought I'd investigate. A good choice, I must say. Don't let me interrupt your workout." He leaned in the doorway, staring at her.

"Not weird or uncomfortable at all," she said.

"I actually have a purpose in remaining here, beyond creepiness."

Paley moved to the rowing machine, turned it on, and started to row. It would be weirder if she didn't work out, and certainly more obvious that he was making her uncomfortable. Which was worse, the fact that he was her boss or the fact that he was a man? They were equally bad, in her mind. "Yes?" she prompted when he remained mute.

"I thought about having a dinner party here next Friday," he said.

"Okay," she said.

He blinked at her. "That's it?"

"What's it?"

"I expected to have to talk you into it," he said.

"Why? This is why you pay me the big bucks, too many of them, if I've never mentioned."

"It's going to be a lot of work," he said.

"Undoubtedly," she agreed.

"There will be eight people, besides me."

"You have enough silverware and plates for twelve," she commented.

"Can you cook for that many people?" he asked.

She paused. "You want me to cook?"

"What else did you have in mind?" he asked.

"I thought you'd want it catered."

"I do. By you," he said.

She frowned.

"Unless that's a problem?" he asked.

"It's not a problem, not in the way you mean. I'm happy to cook for as many people as necessary. It's just…I'm not sure my food is up to snuff for a dinner party."

He folded into a pretzel on the floor beside her. "Paley, are you crazy? Your food is the best. Do you know a group of people now stroll by my office at lunchtime to see what treats come out of the bag?"

She laughed, sure he exaggerated.

"I want you to cook, really, and I'm sure it will be amazing. But I don't want it to be too much for you. And of course I'll pay you extra."

She rolled her eyes. "You already pay me too much, for goodness sake. I would love to do the dinner party for you, if it's really what you want. Although I suggest hiring someone else to wait the table. I'm going to be busy in the kitchen, and I'd feel better if I didn't have to divert my attention in so many directions." She bit her lip. "Is that okay?"

Now it was his turn to roll his eyes. "Of course that's okay. Hire as many people as you want. I'm inviting the partners from my firm, so it's sort of a big deal, and I want it to go perfectly."

She groaned. "No, don't tell me who it is or why they're important. I thought maybe you were doing it to impress a girl, and that's bad enough. But work, gah." She pressed her hands to her ears and shook her head.

He peeled her hands away with a smile. "Fine, it's not for work. It's a group of people I'm dragging in off the street for charity. They've never tasted home-cooked food before, so anything you make will be fine."

"Thank you," she said.

"You're a high-maintenance housekeeper," he said, a lie. She was exceedingly easygoing and mellow, not caring when he made sudden changes in plans that foiled whatever dinner she'd prepped for him.

"And you're a terribly demanding boss," she said, another lie. He seemed happy to let her do whatever she wanted, so long as her work got done, which it always did.

"I guess we deserve each other," he said. He brought his knees to his chest and wrapped his arms around them. He should go. He had taken the day off because he felt burnout approaching. He tended toward workaholism, but he wasn't so far gone he didn't realize when he was headed for disaster. So far he had always been able to pull himself back from the brink, to intervene with some TLC before he became bitter and began loathing his job. It had been harder to keep his distance from work since he and Amelia broke up. This was the first time he'd taken off since everything happened. He planned to read, to catch a movie on TV, maybe even to take a nap. And now he sat on the floor of his basement, watching his housekeeper use his rowing machine, trying not to remember the way she'd looked in her sports bra and shorts. She always wore oversized clothing; he had no idea she had a nice body under all the layers.

"Is there anything special you'd like for supper?" she asked.

"Whatever you think is appropriate for a dinner party," he said.

"I meant tonight," she said. "The world is your oyster. You can eat warm food, fresh from the oven for once."

"You know what I really want?"

"No, that's why I asked," she said.

"I really want pizza from my favorite place. I haven't had it in forever. Since…" Since before he and Amelia broke up. When would he stop viewing his life as one big before and after?

"What do you like on your pizza?" she asked.

"Everything."

"What time should I have it delivered?" she asked.

"They don't deliver," he said.

"What time should I pick it up?" she asked.

"It's in New York," he said, stretching out to lie on his back.

"I'm running out of options here, Mr. Bonvoy."

"I know. I didn't say it was possible; I said it was what I wanted."

"What do you like about that particular pizza so much?" she asked.

"For one thing it's New York style. The crust is big and floppy and chewy and, I don't know, it's sort of perfect."

"Surely we can find a close second around here, if we put our minds to it. I'll do some research, come up with the best option."

"I like that can-do attitude, Paley," Piedmont said, staring up at her from his vantage point on the ground.

"Some problems are easy to solve. The ones that aren't, well, I tend to ignore them," she said. Like her husband, for instance, and the text he'd sent her last night. *We need to talk.* She hadn't texted a reply. Her life was on track, finally. It was like Aaron to sense that and want to torpedo it. If he got her alone, he would likely coerce her to sign things. He had a way of taking the fight out of her, of getting her to acquiesce with no argument, and she didn't trust him. For all she knew, he might try to make her sign on for paying half of his massive student loans, or maybe all of them.

"You're frowning. Are you thinking about pizza?" Piedmont asked.

"No, I'm thinking about student debt," she said.

"You have student debt?" he asked.

"No, I had scholarships and a job."

"What's your degree?"

"English literature."

"Mine, too," he said.

She paused. "I thought it was law."

"My juris doctorate is law. The undergrad can be anything. I like to read."

"What's your favorite?" she asked. "And please know if you say Hemingway, I'm going to have to quit and change my phone number."

"What's wrong with Hemingway?" he asked.

"What isn't? The six-toed cats were really all he had going for him," Paley said.

"I don't have strange, vitriolic dislike of a dead writer like some sad people, but he's not my favorite. I'm more into poetry—Frost, Longfellow, Whitman. Is that okay? Can you remain at your job, working out on company time, you lazy bum?"

"I'll consider it, but I'm going to need a raise," she said.

He laughed. "You're such a weirdo."

"Think how much weirder I'm going to be once you actually get to know me," she said. "Spoiler alert: I once dressed as a TARDIS for Halloween, and I wasn't a child."

He groaned. "A sci-fi geek. I should have guessed."

"Not a sci-fi geek. I just look good in blue," she said, and he laughed. "Why are you judging me when you know what a TARDIS is? Most men don't." Aaron hadn't. She'd had to explain it to him, and he hadn't found it amusing, even though the party she'd gone to had been sci-fi themed.

"I know everything," he replied. "How long are you going to be doing that? You must have rowed across the English Channel by now."

She stopped rowing. "Did you want to use it?"

"No, I just…I don't know. Sorry if that sounded snappish. I felt like I needed a day off, and now all I can think of is everything I need to do at work."

"Are you trying to tell me you need help figuring out what to do with downtime?" she asked.

"That seems over and above your job description," he said.

"No, this is the part Acacia warned me about, this sensing your needs and filling them. If your work wife can do it there, your home wife needs to…no, I don't mean home wife that sounds bad. Housekeeper wife…no, that sounds like we're in a cult. Housewife? Oh, wait, that's already a thing."

"Why don't you take wife out of the equation," he said.

"You sounded so much like my husband just then," she said. He laughed and froze, not sure if he was supposed to. "It's okay. I'm moving out of the crippling grief phase and into the finding pathetic humor in it phase."

"How did you get to that stage?" he asked, half seriously. He still felt as if he were stuck mourning Amelia.

"By reconnecting with my old high school best friend. We laugh at pain, our own and that of others."

"Sounds healthy," Piedmont noted.

"We're fun at parties," she agreed. "Of course we never get invited to any, but I'm sure the two things aren't related."

"Maybe you should stop dressing like a TARDIS for every party," he suggested.

"They'll take my TARDIS costume out of my cold, dead hands," she said. She clapped her hands together. "I'm going to shower. I realize belatedly that by dramatically clapping my hands together before making that announcement, I made it sound as if you were somehow going to be involved. Let me revise; I'm going to shower, and you're going to read. Do you have a book, or would you like me to find something for you?"

"Is that another service you provide?" he asked.

"It's part of the housekeeper code, to edify body, mind and soul through the use of environmentally friendly cleaning products, food, and book recommendations. I had to take a class about it. I got a B because I got flustered on my final and handed a guy a bottle of vinegar and scrubbed the bathroom floor with East of Eden by mistake."

He laughed and rested his forehead on his knees. "This is so bad, Paley. I've spent all my years in DC trying to hide my inner nerd, trying to pretend I'm suave and sophisticated, and you're making me forget all that and remember how much fun it is to be odd and an outsider."

"I don't know what you're talking about. I was cool in high school," she said. "Now, please excuse me while I go put on my TARDIS and shower like other cool, normal people." She left and returned a moment later, book in hand. "This is going to change your life, I guarantee it."

"What if it doesn't?" he asked.

"Then you can lower my salary," she said.

He rolled his eyes and cracked the book.

When Paley checked in on Piedmont forty minutes later, he was fully immersed in the book.

"Well?" she asked.

"Shh, can't talk, reading."

"Come read outside while I work. You're looking a mite pasty, counselor, and sunshine is good for what ails you."

"What do you think ails me?" he asked.

"Currently a lack of sunshine," she answered. She led the way outside. Piedmont settled into a recliner, one he'd forgotten he even possessed, and continued to read. Two hours later, he closed the book and looked around, feeling more than a little as if he had been secretly transported somewhere else during the interim.

"What happened here?" he asked, awed. It was his backyard, but not. Instead it had been transformed into some kind of oasis of every kind of plant and, "Has that tree always been here?"

"No, I planted that so I could make a shade garden with these ferns and lilies," she said, shading her eyes against the sun. She knelt on the ground, dirt up to her elbows and smudged on her nose.

"You really did all this yourself?" he asked.

"Yes. Is that okay?"

"Yes, it's just…it's so pretty. I had no idea it could look this good, nor that I even wanted it to."

"For the record, you're the first person I've ever heard say 'nor' in real life, definitive proof that you are, in fact, a genius," she said.

He didn't answer because he was still too busy taking in the landscape. "This is so…this must have taken forever."

"I told you that you pay me too much for the workload. I spend my copious free time out here."

"Did I pay for all this stuff?" he asked suspiciously.

She squirmed and looked away. "No. I paid for it."

"Paley," he intoned.

"But I love plants, Piedmont. They bring me joy and," she shrugged helplessly, "no offense, but I thought this space could use some."

Piedmont was touched in ways he couldn't articulate. Even though she said she had done it for her, he couldn't help but feel as if she had also done it for him, because she sensed his sadness, because she knew it would make him feel better to have a space like this. He had never been into gardens before, but he was into beauty, usually in the form of art. It had never occurred to him his own yard could be a work of art. "We should get a sculpture," he said.

"I could make one," Paley volunteered. "How do you feel about a bunch of metal hangers twisted together?"

"That's tempting, but I know an art supplier who could find something, if the hangers don't work out."

"Sure, go with the paid professional, play favorites, trample my feelings," she said, returning to her work.

He watched her for a while in silence, admiring the way she became lost in her task. He doubted she even remembered he was there at the moment, and he liked that about her because it spoke of genuineness. He'd encountered a lot of women who played games. Paley was funny and quirky, but she was artless, wholesome, and real.

"How much longer are you going to be doing this?" he asked.

As he had predicted, she jumped and blinked at him as if remembering he was still there. "Why? Do you think I've dug across the English Channel by now?"

"No, but my tummy is rumbly, and I'm hungry."

"Um, let's pause to acknowledge the fact that a renowned litigator used the phrase 'my tummy is rumbly' in everyday conversation," she said.

"Tell anyone, and you'll never dig in this town again," he promised.

"I'm literally shaking. Wait, actually I am. I think I forgot to eat lunch, which means my tummy is rumbly, too." She stood and dusted her hands on her pants. "While I was upstairs getting ready, I did some research. I think I've located some pizza for his worship to try. Let me place the order, and I'll go get it."

"I'll go with you," he volunteered.

"If you're going with me, we might as well eat it there. It's on the other side of DC," she said and paused. "I mean, that was presumptuous, sorry. Maybe you'd rather not eat out." With me, wasn't said, but it was implied.

"Why would I not?" he asked, daring her to answer. Did she think he was a snob?

"Pizza isn't exactly five star cuisine, and you're sort of classy like that," she said, her tone tentative.

"I'm still a twenty seven year old guy, and twenty seven year old guys like pizza," he assured her. "Or so I read in the How to Appear Normal To Others manual I purchased from Amazon."

"Okay, let me get cleaned up," she said. "Back in a jiffy."

He wondered what she meant by "cleaned up," if she would dress up in a bid to impress him. Did she see this as some kind of date? He hoped not; that could be exceedingly awkward. But when she returned, his fears were laid to rest. She had changed into comfortable-looking jeans and a t-shirt with a hoodie tied around her waist. The t-shirt was more form fitting than most of the clothes she wore, and he was momentarily reminded of their earlier encounter in the basement, when she had worn nothing more than a sports bra and shorts. He spun toward the door and stopped short. "I forgot to order a driver."

"I'll drive," she said.

"If we're adding chauffer into the mix, I'm going to pay you more," he threatened.

"Try it, and I'll take the kale and other vegetables out of all your muffins and replace them with butter. Then, when you're mysteriously overweight and dealing with high blood pressure and cholesterol, I'll say, 'ha, I won. You can never beat me.' Then I'll drive you to the hospital because you'll likely have a heart attack or stroke from my surprise victory."

"You've thought about this diabolical plan a terrifying amount," he said.

"The mind tends to wander while rowing and digging," she said.

He sat in the front seat, an odd feeling for him since he was usually in the back seat.

"Why don't you drive?" she asked.

"I do. I mean, I can, I guess I've sort of gotten used to the luxury of being driven. It allows me to do other things, to multitask." Now that he said it out loud, he realized how privileged and spoiled it sounded. He hadn't grown up rich; it was only within the last few years he began making serious money. And now he had a fulltime housekeeper and driver. When had he turned into that guy without even noticing?

"Can I ask you a serious question?" Paley said.

Piedmont tensed, as he always did. "Go ahead."

"Are you going to be mad if this pizza's no good?" she asked, tossing him a smile to let him know she was teasing.

"Furious," he answered. "Why do you always do that to me?"

"Do what?"

"Say you're going to ask something serious and ask something silly," he explained.

"I'm prepping you for the big one. Someday I'll ask you an actual serious question, and you'll be ready."

She found parking a couple of blocks away from the pizza place, and they walked the remaining distance in companionable silence. Piedmont couldn't remember the last time he'd gone for pizza. Even with Amelia, they had ordered in. He frowned, wondering what, if anything, that said about him. Was he becoming too uppity to go to a pizza joint? The crowd he ran with would likely never be caught near such an establishment. Paley was right, they chose restaurants by how many stars were attached and how difficult they were to get into, the more difficult the better. He had liked being with Amelia because she wasn't like that, because she was real and sweet and genuine, unaffected by class and status. But since their breakup, he had fallen into old habits, sometimes feeling as though he spent more time in a tuxedo than out of one. Was that him? Or was he the homespun guy from a small town who happened to have an oversized brain? He never wanted to be the guy who believed his own hype, but he could feel himself slip sliding toward it, toward buying what the press said about The Piedmont Bonvoy, boy wonder, litigator extraordinaire. After the painful breakup with Amelia, the media's rosy assessment of him had been like a balm to his wounded spirit and pride.

He was so deep in his thoughts he didn't realize Paley ordered and paid for them until they were sliding into a booth. "What was that?" he asked.

"That was called a counter. It's where orders are placed," she said.

"No, you paid. Why did you do that?"

"Because dining and dashing is a crime, and I swore they'd never take me back to prison alive."

"Can you give a real answer?" he asked.

"Because why not? Who says I can't pay?"

"Your employer," he said.

"What else am I going to do with my money? Besides save it, obviously. I have nothing else to spend it on." The last part was said a little thoughtfully, a little sadly.

"It's just…"

"I know what it is. It's that you make ten times more than I do, and you feel bad. But when you make less, little things mean more, you know? To you, paying twenty bucks for pizza isn't something you have to think about. But I'm coming from a place where twenty bucks is a big deal, where, at my last job, it was three hours of work for me to get that much."

"But that's my point. Why would you want to spend it on me?"

"Because I get the sense not a lot of people do. Because you seem as sad as I feel. Because you're nice, and I like you. Because even though you're my boss, you sort of feel like a friend. Because you were staring off into space when she gave us the total and it would have been rude to jab you and say, 'Pay, Wallet Monkey.'"

"Please tell me you wouldn't actually have called me, 'Wallet Monkey.'"

"I guess now you'll never know," she said.

"I wasn't born rich," he informed her.

"You seem to have settled in with aplomb."

"Ouch."

"What? That wasn't an insult. I could never fit in the way you do. There must be so many unspoken rules."

"There are," he agreed.

"What's the best part of being nouveau riche?" she asked.

"Actually having money to buy things without that ever-present gnawing worry of homelessness and poverty," he said.

"What's the worst thing?"

"Never knowing if people want to be with me for me or my money and status," he said.

"I get that a lot, too. People invite me over and I get all excited, and then it turns out they want me to clean something for them. I feel so icky and used," she said.

"You're a lying goofball," he said.

Their pizza arrived, and they ate in silence a few minutes, both suddenly desperately hungry. He wondered, as he ate, what went wrong with Paley's marriage. She seemed fun and warm and sweet, totally non-crazy, as far as he could tell. She was cute and could cook. What wasn't to love? On the other hand, having never been married, maybe it was harder than he realized. Maybe the constancy of living with someone, of seeing their sweaty socks in the laundry and hearing them snore night after night, took a toll and began to erode the very foundation of a relationship. Everyone said marriage was hard. If the high divorce rate was any indication, it must be true. And yet people continued to do it. Piedmont himself had wanted to, had even bought the ring. Unfortunately Amelia beat him to the punch, albeit with another man.

He wanted to ask her, all of a sudden, what happened to her marriage. But he couldn't figure out how and still maintain the hands-off fun vibe they'd been sharing. So far the day had been casual, even though they'd spent it fully together. But they had talked about nonsensically silly things, never delving too far into the other's psyche. Tell me about your ruined marriage, was definitely not silly or nonsensical.

Paley received a text, read it with a smile, and responded. "BFF," she replied to his quizzical expression.

"It's hard to take you seriously as an adult when you say, 'BFF,'" he said.

"It's hard to take you seriously as an adult when you have pizza sauce on your cheek," she returned. "What do you call your best friend?"

"Imaginary," he said, scrubbing at the spot of sauce on his cheek.

"I know you have friends; I know you go out," she said, almost accusingly.

"I do have friends; I do go out, but I've never had what you'd call a best friend. The closest I ever came was…" he trailed off, not wanting to mention Amelia.

"A lost love?" she guessed.

He nodded.

"That's sweet-slash-sad." She and Aaron hadn't been best friends. She had been attracted to him, and they'd shared good chemistry, but he had never been to her what Mattie was. That should have been a clue, probably. It occurred to her Mattie and Piedmont would probably get along well. They were cut from the same cloth, both ambitious, smart, hardworking, yet fun and sweet. "You should meet my best friend sometime. I think you guys would hit it off."

He tensed. "That's nice, but I'm not really into fix ups."

She coughed on her sip of soda, nearly spraying the table. He thought Mattie was a girl. "Good to know."

They lingered over pizza a long time, and when they got home, neither knew how to end it. Piedmont usually worked until late and ate a warmed over supper alone. Paley usually read until she fell asleep. They stood awkwardly in the entryway, Paley trying to decide if she should go upstairs to her room or offer to spend more time with him. For the first time all day, she wasn't able to read what he thought or wanted from her.

Piedmont was similarly uncertain. He was reluctant for the day to end, reluctant for the encroaching loneliness to make a return. One of the reasons he threw himself into his job was because he had no reason not to. With Amelia, he had found more balance, more reasons to get away and take time off. Without her, he worked almost incessantly. Today had been a pleasant reminder of what it was like to have a life outside his office, and he was loathe for it to be over.

Finally Paley took a breath. "Do you want to watch a movie in your stately entertainment room? If not, please tell me no and I promise I'll only cry a little and sulk for four days."

"Now that I know what a temptation it is for you to tamper with my food, there's no way I'm saying no. I'll choose the movie, you make some popcorn."

"Yes, sir," she said with feigned meekness. She turned and went toward the kitchen. Piedmont stood still, resisting the urge to follow. Despite what he'd said about her going one way and him the other, the space between them suddenly felt empty. Get it together, Bonvoy, he commanded himself before spinning to head down the stairs.

CHAPTER 11

Paley spent a long time the following week designing a menu for the upcoming dinner party. Everything had to be perfect, not only the flavor and execution of the food, but also the menu itself. These were people who routinely dined at some of the country's finest restaurants. Paley didn't kid herself her food would be as good as those places, but she didn't want to be outlandishly gauche in her attempts to impress. What to her seemed elegant was likely already outdated, a fact confirmed when she studied a few menus from the city's best restaurants. Many of them dabbled in gastronomic feats she wouldn't even attempt. Liquid nitrogen to make instant ice cream? No, thank you. She was a housekeeper, not a chemist.

In the end she stuck with the classics: prime rib, potatoes, green beans, salad, rolls, and chocolate cake. They were the little black dress of dinner party cuisine, and it was hard to go wrong unless she cooked the roast too long. Just in case, she decided to sous vide it so there would be no possibility of overcooking. The problem, she realized on Thursday, was she spent so long planning for the upcoming meal she forgot to hire a waiter, as she had told Piedmont she would. In a panic, she reached for her phone and texted Mattie.

Do you still have the tux you wore to our prom, and are you up for making a quick hundred bucks tomorrow night?

Absolutely yes to both. I assume we're stealing some major artwork. Again. Getting a little old, Anderson.

It's still Marshall, and I'll try to keep the heists to a minimum after this one. I owe you infinity. XO.

Paley sous vide the roast, made the potatoes, and bread dough on Thursday. On Friday morning she baked the cake and set the table. She had ordered a centerpiece from a local florist, so she was off the hook there. The house was already clean, so after frosting the cake she had only to finish the roast, potatoes, rolls, and make the green beans. Mattie arrived with time to spare and she went over the plan with him a few times to make sure he had it right. Everything had to be perfect, and so far everything was. She had no plans to leave the kitchen, but she changed into a skirt, refashioned her hair, and dabbed on some makeup, in case.

Piedmont arrived too late to check on her in the kitchen, but he did send a text.

Everything okay for the party? Need anything last minute?

OH, NO, WAS THAT TODAY?? she texted in reply.

Hilarious. That humor could only be better if you emerge from the kitchen wearing a TARDIS, he said.

takes off TARDIS, puts roast in oven she returned, smiling.

In case I forget to tell you, thanks for doing this. You're a keeper.

A housekeeper, to be specific. She smiled again, imagining him rolling his eyes as he read the text.

"This is all so Upstairs/Downstairs. I love it," Mattie announced, popping an almond from the green beans into his mouth. "The working class heroes in the kitchen, serving the upper crust snobs in the dining room. Bourgeois power." He bumped his fist to hers.

"Your dad is an orthodontist," she reminded him, bumping his fist nonetheless.

"The working man's orthodontist," he replied, picking up a flagon of water and easing his way backwards out of the kitchen.

With Mattie acting as server, Paley was able to focus solely on the food and keep things running smoothly. As soon as everyone had been served, the glasses refilled, cake dished, and coffee poured, Paley and Mattie sat down to pick over what was left.

"When did you get so good at cooking?" Mattie asked, stealing extra roast beef from her plate.

"When I got married and realized the cooking fairy was actually my mom all along and no one was coming to save me," she said.

"The cooking fairy's not real? My entire childhood's been a lie," he said. "Heard from the scuzball again?"

"Two more times, each more urgent. PALEY, I need to talk to you. Paley, I NEED to talk to you. I'm waiting to see if he puts the inflection on each word. Paley, I need TO talk to you. Does that even work? I guess we'll find out."

"What do you think he wants?" Mattie asked.

"Knowing Aaron, probably future rights to one of my kidneys in case he needs a transplant. And, really, that's about all I have left to give."

"I've got a bad feeling. Don't meet with him."

"I won't willingly, but he'll likely track me down. Aaron's not so good at taking no for an answer," she said.

"I could meet up with him in a dark alley sometime, help convince him," he said.

Paley laughed. "Oh, Mattie."

"I'm serious. What? Why are you laughing? I've seen the guy; I could totally take him," Mattie said.

"Thank you for the sweet and odd offer, but I don't want you beating up my husband for me. Please." She rested her hand on his arm.

He picked it up and gave it a squeeze. "Only 'cause you asked so nicely. Otherwise the guy would be toast. Toast, I tell you. I'm very tough."

"You're the toughest bowler I know," she agreed.

The kitchen door opened. Piedmont stuck his head in the door and froze, his eyes darting from Mattie to Paley, their hands still attached. "We're heading outside to enjoy the new and improved back yard, but I wanted to poke my head in and say thank you. The meal was a hit." His eyes rested on Mattie. "Is this your husband?"

"Do I look like a lying, cheating, weasel, lint-licking scuzball tool to you?" Mattie asked.

Paley gave him a reproving tap on the arm. "This is my best friend, Mattie. Mattie, Piedmont Bonvoy, my employer. That intonation was code for 'straighten up.'"

"This is the best friend who stayed over," Piedmont said.

"One and the same," Mattie replied, giving him a Cheshire grin.

"Nice to meet you," Piedmont said, withdrawing from the room before Mattie had time to respond.

"He's so sweet," Paley said.

"What was that?" Mattie hissed.

"What?" she asked, thoroughly confused.

"That look he gave me. He thinks we're a thing."

"Of course he doesn't. He knows I'm in the midst of uncoupling," she said.

"Don't use made up words to sugarcoat it, and I'm telling you he thinks I stayed over for more than practicing contortionism on your loveseat," he said.

"Technically it's his loveseat," Paley said, frowning slightly. Piedmont didn't think she and Mattie were together, did he? If so, was that why he thought her marriage imploded? The thought bugged her, more than a little. She didn't want Piedmont to think badly of her, to wonder if she was the type of person who cheated on her husband.

Mattie volunteered to stay and help her with the dishes, but Paley sent him home with a hundred dollars and a hug. He'd already worked a full day, in addition to playing the part of a waiter for her. He had to be exhausted. And she didn't mind the dishes. They gave her time to think, to assess the evening. If the empty condition of the plates was any indication, the night had been a success. Plus Piedmont told her everyone liked the food.

It was nearly midnight by the time she finished cleaning the kitchen and dining room. The last guest drove away, and Piedmont poked his head into the kitchen again.

"Was there by chance any cake leftover?" he asked.

"Mattie tried to snatch it, but I saved you a piece," she said, sliding it in front of him.

"This cake was extraordinary, Paley, really the whole meal was. I heard many multiple comments on it. Everyone wanted to know the name of my caterer. They about fell off their chairs when I told them my new housekeeper cooked everything."

"Am I blushing?" she asked, pressing her palms to her cheeks.

"Yes, it's cute," he said. "Sit with me."

She sat. "I have to say something that might be a little awkward, but I feel the need to say it anyway. Mattie and I, we're not together. I mean, not in that way. When he stayed over, he actually slept. Nothing happened."

"You're an adult and free to do whatever you want," he said.

"Yes, but I'm a married adult, in the most technical sense of the word. I would never do that while I'm still married. Probably not even afterwards." She stared at a spot on the far wall. "Dating has lost its appeal, possibly forever."

"Someday I have to believe things will get better," he said, sounding as desolate as she felt.

She gave him a sympathetic smile. "Want to talk about it?"

"No." He scraped his plate a few times. "Her name is Amelia. We dated a few months. Things were serious, or so I thought. I bought a ring and planned to propose. Some clients of opposing counsel were troublesome. They kidnapped her and took her to Africa. She married the guy who went after her while they were there."

"Oh, ouch," Paley breathed.

"Yeah. You know what's worse than being dumped? Being dumped for someone you could never be. The guy she married, he's that guy. The conquering hero, basically everything I'm not."

"I should have saved more cake for you," Paley said. "I'm sorry, really, really sorry."

He shrugged. "I'll get over it. Right?"

"You're asking the wrong person."

"What's your story?" he asked.

"Before I worked here, I worked at a bakery decorating cakes. It was a little job, but I loved it. Until the day I decorated my own divorce cake. Turns out my husband of three years had a girlfriend, and now she's pregnant."

"You win," he said.

"It's not a competition, but you're right, I totally win," she said. "And until this moment, I didn't think much about the other woman, but now you've got me wondering. Is she everything I'm not? Is she someone with a power career, someone who has never missed her bus stop because she was caught up in a daydream about talking cats? Someone who doesn't corner the dog at every party and become his constant companion until the night is over? Someone who doesn't even own a TARDIS costume? Someone tall, blond, and willowy?"

"Amelia was tall, blond, and willowy," Piedmont interjected.

"Of course she was," Paley said, sighing. They sat in comfortable silence a few minutes. "Did they really like the food?"

"They loved it. You were a smash."

"Thank you. I know you've worked hard in your career, but when you get offered a partnership, I'm going to claim total credit for it because, despite your years on the job and multiple wins, we both know it was my rib roast and cake that put you over the top."

"For sure," Piedmont agreed, holding his hand aloft for a high five. "Did you pay the waiter?"

"Yes."

"Out of your own money?" he guessed.

"Technically it was your money before you paid me with it," she said.

He gave a longsuffering sigh. "Paley, what am I going to do with you?"

"I spent the last seven days arranging and preparing your fancy dinner party. I think a better question would be what are you going to do without me?" she said.

"Good point. You're getting a bonus."

"That's mean," Paley said, and he laughed.

"And furthermore, I'm sleeping in tomorrow, and I expect you to do the same."

"Define sleeping in," she said.

"Until six."

She gasped. "That's crazy talk. Have you taken leave of your senses? Are you planning to skip your workout too, slacker?"

"No, I thought we'd work out together after whatever fattening breakfast you're planning to make us," he said.

"It's a date, except not really because we've both given up on those. Let's call it an un-date, the kind with no romance and no future, doomed before it even gets off the ground."

"That sounds eerily similar to most of my real dates," he said.

"You should take some hints from my husband. Apparently he's a real ladies' man," she said. She gave his hand a little tap. "Good night, Mr. Bonvoy. May you dream of palm trees and monkeys and no women whatsoever."

"Goodnight, Mrs. Marshall. May your husband soon wake up to realize what a good thing he let go and what an utter fool he's been," he returned.

She gave him a little curtsy, and he laughed. "Go to bed, you weird, weird person."

"Takes one to know one, genius," she replied and scampered out of the kitchen in order to have the last word.

CHAPTER 12

They slept until the appointed time and met up in the kitchen. Piedmont perched sleepily on a stool and watched Paley make breakfast.

"Where are you parents?" she asked.

He blinked confusedly at the interruption of silence. "My dad died my first year out of law school. My mom lives in New Mexico because she hates both DC and cold weather. We're still close and talk several times a week."

"No siblings?"

"Nope. What about you?"

"My parents live in Maryland. We moved here when I was little for my dad's job in human resources at Johns Hopkins. I have an older sister and a younger brother. You'll likely meet my parents when they drop by unannounced at some inopportune time. I've been holding them off with the excuse I need time to settle in, but it won't last forever, so I apologize in advance."

"What's wrong with your parents?" he asked.

"Nothing, they're lovely people. They're just…you'll see."

"Now my curiosity's piqued," he said. "Explain."

"They're in their own little worlds, neither of which intersect with each other, and neither of which mesh with reality. My dad wants order and harmony at all costs, and he believes the best way to achieve it is to keep his lawn perfect. Unfortunately for him he has no idea how to do that so his day is an exercise in futility. My mom is a dreamer. In her world everything is perfect, and she believes the best way to keep it that way is to refuse to allow reality to intrude. She firmly believes the key to making my marriage work is for me to try harder to return to some June Cleaver utopia, to dress better, to make good food, to be always pleasant and never harsh, and to keep the house clean, despite the fact that my husband kicked me out of it and fathered someone else's child. I love them, truly. They are good people and good parents, but too much of a good thing is still too much, and I have to limit myself to small doses for the sake of sanity."

"Are you close to your siblings?"

"Regrettably, no. When you grow up in an environment that disallows talking about real issues, it's hard to form relationships with any depth. We don't talk about things in my house, ever. I needed someone with whom I could be real, could be completely myself and talk about the hard things of life. I found Mattie."

"You and he never dated?"

"We did, briefly our senior year. Didn't take." Her eyes slid away from his and to the table where she rubbed at an imaginary spot. Was it because she had unrequited feelings for her best friend or because he had them for her?

"It must have been hard for him when you got married," Piedmont said.

"He tried to warn me away from Aaron. I thought he was protective, and now I think he was actually correct and I should have listened. But I was young and in love and didn't heed the warning signs." She shook her head. "Sorry, somehow this devolved into a therapy session." The timer on the oven dinged, as if signaling an end to their session. She removed the pan from the oven and refilled their coffee.

"I thought about what you said, about this being an un-date."

"Oh, no, did I make it awkward by trying to make it not

awkward?" she asked.

"No, I agree with you. This is an un-date. Neither of us is in that place where we're looking or ready for romance. Even if we were, there's no guarantee we would…" he paused. "Now I'm making it awkward."

"Pretty much yes," she said.

"Sorry. My point is I need actual dates a lot. I go to seemingly a million black tie events a year, work functions, charity things, galas. Maybe the best part of having a serious girlfriend was that I never had to scrounge for a date. She was a sure thing, and it was amazing and comfortable, actually made dull events fun. Since we broke up, I haven't had the energy to date or look for someone to date. I've been showing up stag, and somehow that's even worse than being on a date with someone I don't like. Picture a wounded zebra in a field of hungry lions. I've never felt so hunted as I have these last few weeks. Last month a woman even followed me into the bathroom. So I thought maybe you could be my standing un-date to these events for the foreseeable future."

Paley remained quiet, thinking. He ate his coffee cake while she pondered. "Would you want me to be merely a friend or pretend to be a girlfriend?"

"I don't know. We'd have to play it by ear. Obviously the truth is best, but I'm not sure that would be enough to deter some of these people and their predatory instincts. My single status is like chum in the water to them. You're laughing at me and thinking I'm being an egotist, but I'm serious. It's crazy. I feel like Mr. Bingley being hunted by all the Bennett sisters."

"I'm sorry, I shouldn't laugh. It must be very hard to be so incredibly desired by all womankind," she said, snickering.

"If it were actually me they desired, I wouldn't complain. But it's not me. I could be anyone. I could have a hump and four arms, and they'd still want me because they want the status and position, the money, the security, even this house." He motioned helplessly to the grand, well-equipped kitchen, and Paley stopped laughing. Women were throwing themselves at him for his kitchen, her kitchen?

"What exactly would my part in this be? What do you need me to be, to do? Do I have to dote and simper?"

He grimaced. "No, please. Never that. Not to complete the misogynist picture of me I'm creating, but basically you need to be arm candy. You need to put on an evening gown, be friendly, smile a lot, and say hello to a whole bunch of strangers. Occasionally we'll dance. It's not horrible, but it's more exhausting than it sounds."

"My evening gown is in the shop," she said.

"I assume Acacia gave you a credit card when you were hired. Use it to buy about five or seven gowns. You could ask her where to do that because I don't actually know. That is, I mean, if you agree to do this."

"I agree," she said, still somewhat solemn.

"Are you sure? I don't want it to seem like this is mandatory or I'm forcing you. In no way will I be upset if you say no," he said.

"I agree of my own will, it's just different from my normal life, so I need to think about it and ponder a while in order to process," she said.

"I get that. Ponder as much as you like, and if at any time in your pondering you change your mind, please tell me. I would so much rather have honesty than feel like I'm dragging you into this."

She put up a hand as if taking an oath. "I solemnly swear to keep you informed and up to date on the slightest passing whims of my mind. I'm thinking chicken for supper tonight, now beef, now chicken. See? You're up to date."

"Great. Now that you've stuffed me with my weekly allotment of butter, are you ready to work out?"

"Yes. Dibs on the rowing machine."

"You're calling dibs on my machine in my house," he reminded her.

"Dibs is a binding and sacred tradition that can't be undone, even with your lawyer voodoo."

"I'm so stealing that line to use in court next week," he said, "but there's another, more time honored tradition you're forgetting."

"What's that?" she asked.

"Race you," he said and took off for the basement.

CHAPTER 13

Paley stood uncertainly on the street. She had been wavering all day, not sure if she could go through with her plan. Tonight was her first time playing Piedmont's date, and she was more nervous about it than she wanted to admit. She didn't want to let him down, to embarrass him in any way. It was that thought that propelled her feet forward.

She opened the door and expected to inhale the familiar chemical smell of salons. Instead she was greeted with the fresh scent of expensive essential oils, along with a well-manicured woman who smiled probingly.

"May I help you?"

"I'd like to speak with Amelia please," Paley said, clearing her throat when her voice came out croaky and uncertain.

The woman's smile dimmed slightly. "I'm so sorry, but Amelia's with a client. May I give her a message?"

"Yes, please. Tell her it's about Piedmont. I'll wait." Paley clasped her arms behind her back and stood still like a soldier at ease. The receptionist left and returned a minute later, followed by a stunningly beautiful blond woman who made Paley feel dowdy and lackluster in comparison. No wonder Piedmont couldn't get over her. She was gorgeous.

"May I help you?" Amelia asked, her beautiful face tinged with equal parts curiosity and confusion.

Paley glanced at the receptionist, still standing eagerly by as if also waiting to hear why Paley was there. "Could we," Paley motioned with her head to the far side of the waiting area. It was only a few feet, but between the noise of the salon and the subtle background music, it would be enough to afford them privacy.

"Is Piedmont okay?" Amelia asked.

"Sort of. It's kind of a long story, I'll make it as short as possible. I'm his new housekeeper. He's asked me to accompany him to some upcoming functions because he doesn't want to have to find a date and he doesn't want to have to go alone."

Amelia's face pinched with equal parts pain and guilt. "Okay. Not to be rude, but what does this have to do with me?"

"Look at me." Paley let her arms gape, revealing her too-big faded sweatshirt and well-worn jeans. "Do I look like the kind of woman who should be on Piedmont's arm at one of these events?"

Amelia didn't answer, but her face said it all.

"I care about Piedmont," Paley continued. "He's been kind to me when I really needed some kindness. You know what he's like; he's a good man. I want to represent well, to make a good showing for him so he doesn't suffer any embarrassment or shame, but I'm clueless to know how to do that. You have insider information, both as his former girlfriend and a stylist. So I came here to blatantly play on any guilt you might have over your breakup with my boss. I know it's unethical to do that, but I'm desperate. Think less harshly of me if you know my desperation is for Piedmont's benefit. I may not get every-thing about his world, but I get that appearances are important. Right now I don't fit at all, but I'm asking you to help me do that. For Piedmont."

Amelia glanced at her watch. "It's going to be tight, but I think I can squeeze you in. What are you wearing?"

"Acacia set me up with a personal shopper. Tonight's gown is spaghetti strap and emerald green."

Amelia tipped her head, apparently trying to envision the gown. "I need to see what your body looks like beneath the behemoth sweatshirt." She took Paley's hand, dragged her to a back room, and ordered her to take off her shirt.

Paley did so nervously, wondering if perhaps it was some kind of trap or prank. The only thing she knew about Amelia was that Piedmont loved her, but what if she was actually mean or a bad person? She stood shivering in her bra and underwear while Amelia walked around her making her inspection. When she was done with that, she tipped Paley's face back and forth in her hand, leaning close to zero in on her face.

"Okay, got it. Put your clothes back on and follow me."

Paley did so without comment. Amelia handed her off to someone who washed her hair, set her in a chair, and massaged her hands. The hand massage worked to ease her anxiety so by the time Amelia returned to her, she was shockingly mellow.

"How's Piedmont doing?" Amelia asked, beginning to brush color onto Paley's hair.

"He's…okay," Paley said.

Amelia's face pinched again. "I didn't mean to hurt him, and I feel terribly about it. My one big regret in life. Piedmont's a good man, but…" she trailed off helplessly.

A picture sat on her station, of her and a man so ridiculously handsome and virile that Paley understood. Even Piedmont, wunderkind, handsome, dashing genius he was, paled in comparison. "That your husband?" Paley asked.

Amelia nodded. "We were friends, and I didn't realize I was in love with him until everything happened. In Africa, it felt worlds away, was worlds away. I forgot myself, forgot everything but him. That's no excuse for hurting someone the way I hurt Piedmont, but it's the best I have to offer. Piedmont and I had a nice relationship, but it doesn't hold a candle to the way things are with Ethan. My only hope is someday Piedmont finds the same and it's that way for him." Her gaze fell speculatively on Paley.

"It won't be me," Paley assured her. "We've become sort of friends, I guess, but I'm having issues of my own. We're more like a lonely hearts club."

"What are your issues?" Amelia asked.

Paley began to wonder if there was some sort of magic about being in a salon chair because, despite her best intentions, she began spilling her heart to Amelia, about Aaron's mistreatment and betrayal, including the cake he'd ordered announcing their divorce. Amelia clucked sympathetically and frowned, and it was soothing somehow to talk to someone who was on her side.

"So that's where Piedmont entered the picture. I live in the third story maid's quarters now, and we sort of hang out and keep each other company, to assuage our combined misery." She glanced at Amelia. "Sorry. I'm not actually trying to make you feel guilty."

"Aren't you?" Amelia asked with a wry smile.

"Okay, maybe I disliked and blamed you before I met you, but I can see you're a nice person who didn't mean to hurt Piedmont. But I also see the other side of it. Piedmont's hurt, and that's hard."

"Especially because you're facing your own hurt and betrayal. It's okay, go ahead and be on Piedmont's side. I'm the one doing okay here. He needs you."

"You're irritatingly nice and rational," Paley commented. They shared a smile in the mirror.

After putting some artful highlights and lowlights in her dishwater blond hair, Amelia also did Paley's makeup. Paley had thought she would look a little more put together. She hadn't expected to look like an entirely different person. She stared at herself, dumbstruck, Amelia crossing her arms behind her with what could be considered a smug expression.

"Didn't think you had it in you, did you?" Amelia asked.

Paley shook her head, speechless.

"Everyone does, it needs a little coaxing to come out sometimes," Amelia said. She gave her a brief lesson on the makeup and referred her to her YouTube tutorials for further help. Paley reached for her purse.

"I intended to pay you, in case I didn't make that clear from the beginning. I wasn't asking for a freebie, only for you to fit me in. I know you're backlogged."

"No. This one's on the house, for Piedmont."

"He'll never know I was here," Paley said.

"But he'll get to enjoy my work, and that will bring me untold satisfaction and release," Amelia said.

"He doesn't think of me that way," Paley assured her.

Amelia remained silent, not wanting to interfere and mess anything up. But she knew Piedmont, and she had her suspicions. "Do me a favor and send me a picture of the final result with the dress."

"Okay," Paley said. She dithered uncertainly. "Would it be weird if I hugged you?"

"Yes," Amelia said, but opened her arms and gave Paley a tight hug anyway. "Take care of him. He's a good man."

"I know, and I'll do my best."

Paley drove home, trying hard not to dart looks at herself in the mirror. She'd had her hair and makeup done both for prom and for her wedding, but she had never looked this good. Both of those times, the salons had made her up, had made her look like someone else. This time she could still see herself in the makeover, but it was in a way she had never seen herself before, as if all the natural beauty she'd been hiding had been unleashed. Even better, she thought she could attain the look on her own. Suddenly she wanted to ditch Piedmont's event and go shopping. Amelia had told her to burn the oversized hoodies, suggesting instead a few form fitting pieces in colors designed to enhance her features. She couldn't wait to follow through and buy them. Tomorrow, she promised herself. She hadn't shopped in forever, and she was long overdue for a wardrobe refresh. Thanks to Piedmont's blatant overpayment, she had plenty of money on hand to do that now.

Though she had been putting on a good front for Piedmont, she had been rather dreading the coming outing, sure she wouldn't fit in, would embarrass him, wouldn't be able to pull off what she needed to do. She still might mess it up but, thanks to Amelia, she at least now looked the part. No one looking at her tonight would guess she was the maid, would realize how thoroughly she didn't belong. That was all she wanted, for Piedmont not to be embarrassed by her.

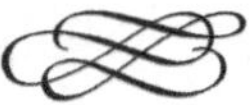

Piedmont was likewise having second thoughts. Not that Paley would embarrass him. Though she usually dressed down in jeans and hoodies, he knew she'd talked to Acacia who had set her up with a proper dress. What he regretted was the possibility that he had complicated and potentially messed up the odd relationship between them. They were boss and employee. They also had a budding friendship. Both of those things felt tenuous and in need of protection. In an era of #MeToo, was he some kind of fool for inviting his housekeeper on what could only be described as a date? And Paley was fragile right now. She said she understood this was an un-date, but did she really? Had he been clear that he had no intentions other than needing what amounted to an escort? And was it bad he had asked his paid employee to be his escort? Was there something unethical about that? He had offered to pay her extra, and she had laughed in his face.

He felt jittery as he stood at the base of the stairs, tugging at the seemingly too-tight collar of his tux as he waited for Paley to descend. She wasn't usually late, but they had to leave in approximately thirty seconds, and she still hadn't made an appearance. He stared at his watch, wondering if he was going to have to call her to come down, when suddenly she was there, standing on the bottom step and tapping his shoulder.

He turned to look at her with a smile that immediately fled as his jaw dropped and lingered. Except for the day he saw her in her sports bra and shorts, he had only ever seen her in jeans and an oversized t-shirt or hoodie. If he hadn't seen her in her workout gear, he would have guessed she was much heavier than she actually was because he was used to seeing her in baggy clothing. Her hair was always up in a ponytail or bun, her face free of makeup. But tonight... If he didn't know it was her, he wouldn't have known it was her. She wore a floor-length spaghetti strap dress that showed off shoulders that had apparently been toned from so many hours on his rowing machine. Her hair was longer than he realized, falling below her shoulders in soft waves, looking richer and blonder than he remembered. And her face was...had her eyes always been green? Her lips always so full and pink?

"We should go," he watched the lips say. Her voice was the same, and it brought him back from wherever he'd been. He snapped into focus and held out his hand to her.

"You look great." Understatement. She looked incredible, as good as any woman he'd seen at any of these events. He had wanted a date who would blend in, would be an anonymous side note to him in order to keep him off anyone's radar. But Paley would no doubt stand out, and he wasn't at all certain how he felt about that. He glanced at her again, feeling a bit protective. Other men would see her and be attracted to her, and she was nowhere near ready for that. He would need to keep close to her, to ward others away.

"I don't think I've ever seen you in your tux before. You look dashing," Paley said, touching her finger to the bowtie at his neck.

"Bonvoy, Piedmont Bonvoy," he said, adjusting his tie.

"I prefer Jason Bourne," she said.

"Most women do," he said, his tone sinking.

"Then most women don't know what they're missing," she said, resting her hand on his and giving it a gentle squeeze. He kept the hand, tucked softly in his as they rode in the back seat on their way to the event. Otherwise they didn't talk or have contact, each of them staring out a window, lost in thought.

Paley was nervous and trying not to be. Amelia had also coached her on how to behave, and she would be eternally grateful. For almost everyone a smile and polite hello will be enough. If you find yourself lost and grasping for topics, ask if they have a boat or a horse. Lots of rich people do, and they like to talk about them. When in doubt, ask a question. People of all walks of life like to talk about themselves. Paley catalogued a mental inventory of pertinent questions and hoped she'd be able to remember them when the time came.

For his part, Piedmont remembered how it was with Amelia, how they rode in this car the same cozy way, how she had so effortlessly charmed everyone she encountered. He thought he had found the perfect person for him, but for the first time in his life he hadn't been enough. There had been someone better, and it stung. Deeply.

All too soon they were there.

"We have to get out of the car," Piedmont said when neither of them made a move to leave.

"You first," Paley said.

"Why am I nervous? I've done this before," he said. He stepped out of the car and held his hand for her. She took it and eased out, taking a deep breath. "We only have to stay a little bit. If it's bad, we'll go."

"It won't be bad; it will be fun," she declared.

"Clearly you've never been to one of these events if you think it will be fun," he said.

Her eyes sparkled with mischief. "That sounds like a challenge."

"It's not a challenge; it's a statement. These events are droll and boring, never fun."

"Challenge accepted," she said, and set her face toward the ballroom.

They were smiling as they walked in. Paley was unaware of the many, many eyes on them, but Piedmont knew. Curiosity about her would go into overdrive. He should have warned her, but there was no real way to prepare for it. Paley, oblivious to the new attention, glanced around the room and leaned in to whisper.

"I hoped for a karaoke machine."

Piedmont snickered at the thought of DC's elite belting Elton John on karaoke. "It's in the shop," he whispered in return. "I told you fun's impossible here."

"Unlikely does not equal impossible," she said and resumed scanning the room. The crowd schmoozed. Even though Paley had never seen it before, she had no trouble recognizing it. Everyone tried to be the biggest, the best, the richest, the most important. Piedmont didn't seem like that sort of person to her, but then she'd never seen him in a professional setting before. Maybe she was about to see a new side of him, a side she wouldn't like.

He led her to a group of people who opened to them with calculated smiles. "Piedmont," an older man said, sticking out his hand to shake. "And who is your lovely date this evening?"

"Paley Anderson," she said, sticking forth her hand without waiting for Piedmont to make the introduction. Was she supposed to do that? No one looked at her askance for being forward. The man took her hand and shook it.

"Paley, this is Arthur Andrews, the senior partner at my firm," Piedmont offered.

"Ah, the chocolate man," Paley said, smiling.

Arthur blinked at her in confusion.

"Piedmont let me taste some chocolate you brought back to the office from Belgium, and it was incredible, so now you're forever linked with chocolate in my mind. In case you can't tell, that's a good thing. Although, in telling you this story, I realize I divulged that Piedmont stole some of your chocolate and smuggled it home. Please don't fire him on my account."

Arthur laughed a bit uncertainly, as if not sure what to make of her. "Piedmont would have to smuggle a lot more than chocolate to make me fire him. And I'll make sure and send you some chocolate. I bought too much of it."

"Too much chocolate? That's impossible," Paley said.

"Paley's a baker," Piedmont said, linking his arm with hers.

"He's trying to explain away my inordinate interest in chocolate, but I've always been this way," Paley said, then realizing she was talking too much about herself, added, "Was this your first trip to Belgium?"

Arthur launched into a few stories about Belgium and someone else took over the conversation. Piedmont led her to another group of people. "I'll try not to focus on chocolate," she whispered.

"You're doing fine," he assured her and meant it. Arthur had been a bit baffled by her, but that was a good thing. He liked things that were unusual, and a woman who blurted passionate feelings on chocolate and made him laugh was definitely unusual.

He realized where he had led her and immediately almost led her away before the woman started talking. "Who's your friend?" she asked.

"This is Paley…Anderson." Apparently Paley was using her maiden name for the night, a fact he needed to remember. "Paley, this is Patricia Von Puffington."

He could see the laughter building. Don't do it, don't do it, he mentally pled with her. She grasped his bicep and dug her nails painfully into his arm. "It's so delightful to meet you," she said at last, extending her free hand to Patricia. She wouldn't make eye contact with him, and he was glad. If their eyes met, one of them would laugh. The way he currently felt, it might be him. He had always thought Patricia's name was hilarious, but no one had ever shared his amusement over it. Instinctively he knew Paley would, and he was correct. She kept a straight face throughout the entire conversation, but after it was over she led them behind a heavy velvet curtain and laughed. Hard.

"I mean, seriously," she said, wiping her eyes. "Von Puffington, come on. Did my mascara run?"

"A tiny bit," he said using his thumbs to wipe away the faint smudges. When his hands touched her face, a buzz of electricity bounced between them, at least it did on his end. She seemed oblivious to it, to his touch.

"We should probably get back out there before anyone notices our disembodied feet sticking out beneath the curtain," she said.

"They'd probably assume we're making out," he said.

"Do people do that at these events?"

"Last year I caught Patricia Von Puffington and Clouse McClown-ington going at it behind the punch bowl," he whispered, and she doubled over laughing, her hand grasping his arm for support.

"Stop it, I just got it out from the last attack." She straightened and took a few deep breaths. "No one is actually named Clouse McClown-ington, is there?"

"No, but there's a Biffy and a Rover out there somewhere, so prepare yourself."

She snorted but kept herself in check. "That's going to be our game for the night, to make up rich people nicknames for everyone we encounter." She touched his shoulder. "And go." They emerged from behind the curtain, apparently undetected, and moved on to the next group of people to converse with. Halfway through, while conversation swirled around them, Paley leaned over to whisper in Piedmont's ear. "Scheherazade Floofington and Bennington Fingerbiscuits," in regard to the two people monopolizing the conversation. Piedmont choked and pulled Paley away to the drink table.

"Are you trying to kill me?" he asked.

"Did you see his hands? Guy had literal finger biscuits. His nail beds looked like drumsticks, and he kept motioning as he talked about yacht club. I got a sudden craving for waffles."

"Why waffles?" Piedmont asked.

"Chicken and waffles."

He gave her a blank look.

"You've never had chicken and waffles?"

"No, but it sounds disgusting," he said, grimacing.

"Okay, lunch tomorrow, and you'll see."

They were still by the long bar when the next boring conversation found them. Once again it swirled around them as they nodded with forced politeness. This time it was Piedmont who leaned close and whispered. "Butterlicious Vanderbilt and Velvet Bordeaux."

"Of the Louisiana Bordeaux," Paley added, and they both had to excuse themselves to laugh.

For the rest of the night, they were lost in their own little world of nicknaming the boring people around them. It was, hands down, the most fun Piedmont ever had at such an event. By the time they piled back into the car, his face hurt from laughing.

"This feels like prom," Paley noted.

"I wouldn't know. I was twelve when I was in high school," he said.

"I love how you can bandy that about without sounding pompous," Paley said. "On the other hand, it makes me sad you never got to experience prom or after prom."

"What's after prom?"

"Pregnancy, for some," she said, and he laughed, pressing his palms to his aching cheeks to stop the pain. "For me it was bowling."

"This is the part of the evening where I sound like a total snob and reveal I've never been bowling."

Her jaw dropped. "Are you even...?" She leaned forward and gave Charles a new location. "It's time to end this," she added sitting back.

"Are you going to kill me? Take me to non-bowler's prison?"

"No, but tonight you'll lose your bowling virginity," she declared.

"Okay, but I hope you brought protection because I didn't come prepared," he said.

"A little antifungal spray in the shoes, and you're covered," she promised.

"Somehow I feel I'm not the first man you've said that to," he said.

"Well, I was married," she said and frowned. "And I still am."

"Basically you're a bowling tease," he said.

"Not hardly. Teases only talk. I always follow through. See, that's actually a bowling term, so if you knew that, it would be funny," she said.

"Somehow I doubt it," he said, and she laughed. "Can I bowl in a tux?"

"There's really no other way," she said.

The bowling alley was surprisingly crowded for midnight. "Are you sure we can get a lane?" Piedmont asked.

"It's okay, I have an in with the owner," Paley assured him. She took his hand and wove him through the cars and to the entrance, standing aside so he could open the door for her. Once inside, he expected heads to turn at their overdressed appearance, but no one seemed to notice them, save the man in charge.

Mattie stood behind the counter, staring at Paley openmouthed. He leapt the counter with a surprising amount of gracefulness, as if it were a practiced move, and came to greet them.

"Paley Anderson, as I live and breathe. I thought you were too good for the likes of my bowling alley."

"I am, but for tonight I'm setting aside my golden toilet brush, coming down from my third floor maid quarters, and gracing your establishment with my presence," she said. She bestowed her hand royally to him. He bowed and kissed it.

"I'm extremely hopeful you've washed this since the last toilet you cleaned," Mattie said.

"Some water splashed out, so it's practically the same thing," Paley said. She rested her hand on Piedmont's bicep. "Prepare yourself for something shocking, Mattie. Piedmont's never bowled before."

"I could have guessed that about him," Mattie said, turning to Piedmont with a blank expression.

"It's not his fault. He grew up in Luzbeckistan, and they outlawed bowling in 1973. So really, this is like Footloose and you're Kevin Bacon to his John Lithgow."

"Stop it, you know my secret dream of being Kevin Bacon," Mattie said. "Duty calls me, but help yourselves to whatever. Lane three is about to open." He rested his hand on Paley's head. "I take it you can teach him our ways."

"I'll do my best," Paley promised.

"I have full confidence in you. Also, literally never seen you look better." He kissed her cheek and disappeared somewhere within the building, Piedmont never actually saw where.

Paley took his hand. "Are you ready? Your life will never be the same after this. When you go to more of your fancy soirees, the Von Puffingtons of the world will know you've bowled, they'll smell it on you, probably literally because it's really hard to get this stench out of clothes. From this point on, there's no turning back."

He thought there was probably some truth in that, and he didn't peer too closely into what it might be. Instead he gave her hand a squeeze. "Teach me your ways, I beg you."

Paley put his hand on her shoulder and led him to lane three.

CHAPTER 15

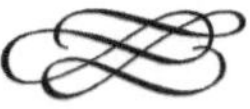

After that night, they continued to go to Piedmont's events, but something new sprang up between them.

"What else haven't you done?" Paley asked on the way home from bowling.

"I've never walked on the moon, never been to Mars," Piedmont said.

"No, I mean normal things like bowling."

"If I haven't done them, how would I know they're normal?" he asked.

"See, it's reasoning abilities such as those that will make you partner in no time," she said, and he smiled. He was tired, but it was a good kind of tired, more than the usual exhaustion from having to be "on" all night. His instinct to invite Paley had been correct; she had made the evening more than the bearable he'd been expecting. With her, it had been fun, the most fun he'd had in recent memory.

"I'm going to have to make a list," she said, alerting him to the fact that he'd dozed.

"Check it twice, find out who's naughty and nice?" he guessed.

"Have you ever been Christmas caroling?"

He shook his head.

"That's going on my list," she said, her tone cryptic.

"What list?" he repeated.

"The list of normal things you missed out on by being a genius. Jumped on a trampoline?"

He shook his head.

"Played hide and seek in the dark?"

He shook his head.

"Wow," Paley said. "I'm going to have to put some thought into this."

"Kay," he said, only half listening. He rested his head on the seat, and the next thing he knew they were home and she tapped his shoulder.

"Piedmont, we're here," she whispered.

"Where?" he asked, momentarily confused.

"We're home," she said, and his heart turned over unexpectedly. It was his home, yes, but it was hers too, and she had made it such with her warm presence, her brimming garden, her laughter, her hot meals and fresh baked treats, the thousands of thoughtful little things she did for him that he probably didn't even notice. All of a sudden he realized she was the best friend he had, which was kind of sad really, given she was his employee.

"I'm glad you're here, Paley," he whispered.

"Me too," she said, smiling.

Piedmont felt it again, the little spark of electricity between them. He wondered if she also felt it this time because her expression clouded, her smile disappeared.

"I forgot to set the chicken out of the freezer," she whispered, and he laughed. "What? Why is that funny?"

"Nothing. I'm slaphappy, I guess. It is three in the morning, after all."

"And you have to get up in an hour to work out," she noted.

He groaned. "You're making me a lazy night owl."

"I'll skip the Saturday pastry tomorrow," she offered.

"Do and you're fired," he warned.

"You say that so often it's starting to lose meaning." They stared at the house, each of them loathe to leave the cozy warmth of the car.

"I guess we'd better let Charles go to sleep, too," Piedmont said, referring to his driver.

"He's probably fine, he slept all the way home," Paley said, and Piedmont smiled at her.

"Thanks for tonight, Paley. It was fun."

"You mean it was unexpectedly fun," she surmised.

"Yes. These events are usually tedious, but tonight was different."

"According to you, we have a few more coming up. We'll have to see if we can make tonight the new normal."

Suddenly Piedmont found himself looking forward to the future, more than he had at any time since before Amelia. Maybe it was going to be okay; maybe eventually he'd get over her and life would resume and the hole in his heart would go away or fill up or whatever might make it better, make him better.

Somehow they had started spending their weekends together unspoken. On Saturday mornings they slept later than usual, had a leisurely and fattening breakfast, and worked out. After that Piedmont followed Paley to the garden and read while she dug in the dirt or weeded. At night Paley made supper or they ordered pizza and watched a movie in the entertainment room downstairs. It was the first time in his life Piedmont had ever really hung out doing nothing. He'd had no friends in school, thanks to his odd age at the time, always different from everyone else in every school he'd ever attended. His friends now were colleagues who were all decades older, so he still didn't fit. Amelia had been too busy to hang out. She worked long hours at the salon and had her sister and friends, so when they saw each other, it was usually at one of his events where she was his date. He began to wonder if perhaps his relationship with her hadn't been as deep or as solid as he'd believed. She had been twenty two, five years younger than him, and yet they had never once lounged on the couch and watched mindless TV, the way he and Paley did.

"Is this what you and your husband did together?" he blurted one night. He was looking for a frame of reference, trying to understand what was normal and realizing, surprisingly for the first time, that he wasn't.

"In the beginning. I like to go out, but I also need time at home, to recoup and regroup, to refuel. Aaron always wanted to be on the go. When we were first dating, he was happy to spend some nights at home with me, and I was happy to go out some nights with him. We had a good balance. Somewhere along the way that shifted. I started staying home alone every night, and he started going out alone all the time. I don't know how or why. Did I start refusing to go or did he stop asking me?" She shook her head. "Either way, it's been nice to get out again." She patted his knee and gave him a smile.

"It's been nice to stay in," Piedmont agreed. Being with her was a reason not to work, and he was thankful for that. He didn't need a psychiatrist to tell him there was more to life than a job, and he was on his way to major burnout if he didn't make a change. Paley provided that change; she gave him something to do with his downtime, helped him learn how to relax and unwind. He'd read more in the last few weeks than he had since the textbooks he read for law school.

"Having said that, I think we should go out tomorrow," she said.

"Where?" he asked.

"Mattie and my brother helped me come up with a list of normal experiences you should have had by now. We're going to work our way through them."

"Why again?"

"So you won't have regrets when you're ninety," she said.

"You really think I'm going to be ninety and regret never jumping on a trampoline?" he asked.

"Now you'll never have to face that question," she said. "Shh, this is my favorite part."

"Other employees don't tell their bosses to 'shh,'" he said.

"Shh," she reiterated, pressing her palm to his mouth.

He was tempted to kiss it, but he didn't. So far their friendship had remained purely platonic. Piedmont was reluctant to break that, for both their sakes. They needed each other, needed their friendship. Whether they would someday need more than that remained to be seen. For now, this was enough. In fact, this was everything. So he pushed her hand away, rested his head on the couch, and tried to pay attention to the movie and not to her.

Was she wearing new clothes? He thought so, and he tried not to wonder why. These clothes fit her, highlighting what he had confirmed was a nice figure. Don't think about her figure. How can I not think about her figure when it's pressed against my arm, all warm and soft and good smelling? Don't think about how she smells. Stop telling me not to do things in regards to her. You're hopeless. Shut up.

"If you fell asleep during the middle of this movie, we can't be friends," Paley said, poking him.

He opened his eyes, regretting it immediately when she was mere centimeters from his face.

"I'm not asleep."

"Your eyes were closed."

"I was talking to myself," he said.

"Are you a supreme being that you have to do that with your eyes closed?" she wondered.

"You said supreme, and now I'm hungry for pizza," he said.

"We're having chicken and waffles," she declared.

"You know I'm paying you. I'm supposed to be the one who chooses the menu," he said.

"It's Saturday, I'm off the clock, and I'm making you chicken and waffles," she said.

"Let me tell you in Latin all the ways that argument went wrong," he said, and she pressed both palms to his lips, knocking him over in her effort to reach him. She landed on his chest, and his hands rested automatically on her hips.

"Okay, that did not turn out as I intended," she said. She removed her hands from his mouth and quickly sat up away from him. Before Piedmont could comment, her phone buzzed with a text. She read it and tossed it away with a huff.

"Not Mattie, I take it," he said. Whenever it was Mattie, she smiled like she'd gotten a letter from Santa. Piedmont tried and failed not to be jealous of that look.

"Aaron," she said.

"What did he say?"

"The same thing he always says. That he needs to meet with ME." She smiled and shook her head.

"Whatever it is, refer it to your lawyer," Piedmont said.

"I would, if I had one."

He faced her. "You're in the midst of a divorce, and you don't have a lawyer?"

She shook her head.

"Paley."

She jumped at his sharp tone. "He said I didn't need one."

"Your husband told you that you didn't need a lawyer for the divorce he foisted on you, and you believed him?"

"I know it was stupid." She rubbed her forehead and closed her eyes. "I wasn't in a good place when it first happened, I didn't think clearly."

"You're going to think clearly from now on," he said. He removed his phone and began to text. "Who is his lawyer?"

"I don't know, maybe himself."

He froze and looked at her again. "Your husband is a lawyer?"

"Did I not mention?"

"No, you did not mention. Do I know him?"

"I doubt it, he's new, barely out of law school. He certainly knows you," she said, giving him a smile that was fully amused now.

"I bet he does," Piedmont agreed. "And he's about to know me better."

"What are you doing?" she asked.

"Asking one of my friends to handle your case. He's the premier divorce attorney on the east coast. By the time he's finished with your husband, he'll be selling his plasma to afford oats for breakfast."

"I don't want that, really. I only want what's fair."

"Did you work and support him while he was in law school?" Piedmont asked with his lawyer voice, the one that demanded she answer immediately with the truth or so help her.

"Yes."

"Then, baby, everything is fair." He sent his text, received one in reply, and smiled. A minute later, her phone beeped with another text from Aaron.

You got a lawyer?? How are you affording Ashley Benholt?

"Is my lawyer's name Ashley Benholt?" she asked.

"Yes," Piedmont answered absently. He glanced over her shoulder, shamelessly read the text from Aaron, then snatched the phone out of her fingers and sent one in reply. Now it was Paley's turn to read it over his shoulder.

Please direct all further discourse to my lawyer.

She whistled appreciatively. "You don't mess around, Piedmont Bonvoy."

"Nothing's too good for my maid," he declared. "Now go order me a pizza."

"Chicken and waffles," she said, reaching for the remote.

"You vex me, Paley, you really do," he said, but when she settled back against the cushion, he rested his head on hers, a smile of contentment on his face.

CHAPTER 16

"I really am sorry," Paley repeated for the hundredth time.

"So you said," Piedmont replied shortly.

"Honestly, Piedmont, I couldn't have predicted you would get hit in the face," she said. She reached out to touch his shiner, but he moved out of reach.

"How am I supposed to tell my colleagues I got a black eye from the batting cages? I'm going to have to wear makeup in court," he said. They had spent the afternoon at her behest, scratching another thing off the list of normal activities she'd prepared for him. The batting cages had been fun until Piedmont took a ball to the face. Now they were on their way to a charity gala. Paley looked perfect again, but Piedmont's eye was angry, purple, and swollen.

"I think it's fetching, like a pirate," Paley said.

"You are a bad liar," he groused. More than his ridiculous appearance, the pain made him cranky. Paley had spent the afternoon babying him with ice packs and aspirin, but the movement of getting dressed in his tux had made the injury throb, and now he was grumpy.

"I'm really sorry," Paley muttered weakly, and he felt bad for being so short with her. He opened his mouth to tell her so, but the car stopped and Charles opened the door for him.

"Think of it as a trophy," Charles chimed in. "Guys get those." Charles was a decade older and, though also on Piedmont's payroll, saw himself as something of a big brother. "And give her a break," he added in a whisper. "She meant well."

Piedmont gave him a nod, his face aching with the movement. He came around the car and reached for Paley's hand, but her arms were crossed over her chest. Protectively or angrily, he wasn't certain. He held the door for her, and they stopped short in the entryway. She fished in her purse and handed him a small bottle.

"It's time for more aspirin. Why don't you go to that drinking fountain down the hall? I'll wait here."

He took the bottle and disappeared. Paley let out the breath she'd been holding. She felt terrible. All she'd wanted was for Piedmont to have some fun. He worked so hard; he deserved to let loose a little in his downtime. But now he had a swollen black eye he'd have to parade in front of his colleagues, and it was all her fault.

"Paley?"

She heard Aaron's voice and froze, her insides immediately going numb. Slowly, she turned to face him and he blinked at her in shock. She'd lost fifteen pounds since she saw him and gotten a makeover. His face reflected that, and so much more.

"You can't be here," he whispered furiously.

"What?" she asked, not understanding what he was saying. "Why not?"

"Because it's by invitation only, and it's for lawyers."

"Lawyers and their guests," she said.

"You're not my guest," he said, shaking his head. "I never dreamed you'd be this desperate, dressing yourself up, sneaking in here. I've been begging to meet with you, and now I see why you've been avoiding me. It's because you were trying to make yourself presentable. But it's over, Paley. I've moved on."

Paley stood still, unable to fathom a reply.

"Ready, sweetheart?" Piedmont came up beside her and took her hand, giving it a squeeze that brought her back to the present. She tore her eyes off Aaron and rested them on him. The pain in them made him flinch, made him murderously angry at the man who put it there.

"Yes," Paley said, blinking a few times to try and clear eyes now swimming with tears. They turned their backs on Aaron, and he led her away without waiting for any sort of introduction.

"Let's dance," Piedmont said, leading her onto the floor.

"No one's dancing yet," she said.

"No law says we can't be the first."

"The first people on the dance floor are always the weirdos," she said.

"That fits us then," he said, pulling her close and leading her in a dance that didn't leave them much opportunity to speak. "So that's your husband, he seems nice," he said when the second dance began. "I'm really wondering what you saw in him."

"Me too," she said. "He's handsome."

"So are poison dart frogs," he said. She giggled, and he smiled.

"Thank you for the rescue," she said.

"My pleasure and, hey, I have some good news."

"What's that?"

"Thanks to our combined attendance at these events, people are going to tell him we're a thing, when he asks."

"What makes you think he'll ask?" she said.

"He'll ask," Piedmont assured her. He knew the type. He wanted to believe Paley was devastated over him. He enjoyed hurting her, breaking her heart. It made him feel like a big man. To know he hadn't succeeded, that Paley was doing well and moving on, would kill him.

"You're smiling," Paley said.

"I am. And I'm sorry I was grumpy with you earlier."

"That's okay. I really am sorry about your eye."

"It's a badge of honor," he said, drawing her slightly closer. She shifted her hands sliding them around his neck.

"A man with a black eye, when it wasn't gotten by ill gains, is kind of sexy," she whispered.

"What's considered ill gains?" he asked.

"Clocked in the face by an old lady he tried to mug," she supplied.

"Good thing you told me; that was going to be my cover story," he said, and she laughed. "And the day was fun, despite the shiner. Soon you're going to make me into a real boy."

"Call me Geppetto."

"No."

She laughed again.

For the remainder of the night, she felt Aaron's eyes on her, but she didn't turn to look until once, by accident, she caught sight of him in her peripheral. A woman stood beside him. Unbidden, Paley's eyes turned in their direction, and she wished they hadn't. The woman was adorably cute with a pregnant belly that extended far from her body. A jolt of shock ran through Paley, followed quickly by pain. Piedmont was mid-conversation but still somehow sensed Paley's shudder. He turned, caught sight of where she was looking, and leaned down to whisper.

"She has cankles."

"I think you're supposed to when you're that far along," Paley said, trying and aiming for a light tone.

"Nah, she had them before. I can tell, I'm kind of a connoisseur of ankle proportion. Yours are perfect, by the way." He gave her shoulder a light squeeze, earning a genuine smile.

"Ankles, really? That's what you're into?" she whispered.

"Among other things," he replied, giving her another squeeze.

She linked her arm with his. "You're nice."

"That's because you've never opposed him in court," the person standing across from them said after having caught the last part of their conversation.

"All in due time," Paley said.

"Oh, no. I wouldn't face you, not after you beat me on the chicken and waffles thing," Piedmont said. After making him eat them, he realized he liked them, loved them, in fact.

"Well, love is the most powerful weapon, or so they say," their conversational interloper said. Paley and Piedmont didn't comment, and they studiously avoided eye contact for a while after.

"What happened to the eye?" one of the senior partners asked

Piedmont, catching sight of his shiner. It was Brewster Adams, the most crotchety and standoffish partner, one Piedmont had never been able to warm up to.

"Baseball."

"You play?" Brewster asked, perking up with interest.

"Not well, apparently," Piedmont said with a self-deprecating smile.

"Even so, you should join the firm's league. Good or not, you'd be the only member with your original knees."

"I'll give it some consideration," Piedmont said, knowing no matter what he would do it. If baseball bridged the gap between him and the partner who would likely have the final say on his own partnership, he would be willing to become a baseball and be hit with a bat.

"Remind me to pick up some books on baseball," Piedmont whispered to Paley as they walked away.

"I think we can do better than that," Paley whispered, patting his arm.

"Why do I feel a sudden chill?" he asked.

"You'll survive," she said. "Mostly."

CHAPTER 17

Later that night they were sitting on the couch in the basement, drowsily watching a movie. Even Paley had trouble staying awake, and Piedmont was already out. She should wake him to go to bed, but the movie was nearly done. She would finish it, and then they would go upstairs. In the meantime her blinks were becoming longer and longer, and then she sat up in alarm.

Had that been a beep? The same beep that happened whenever someone opened an outside door? Her ears strained as she leaned toward the basement's opening. Overhead a board creaked. Paley knew that board; it was the same one in the kitchen she stepped on every day.

Frantically, she shook Piedmont awake, then covered his mouth and pressed her lips to his ear. "I think someone's in the house and heading this way," she whispered.

He blinked at her, sat up, took her hand, and herded her into a closet, all while pulling out his phone and hitting a button.

"Lights off," he said into the phone, and everything went black. He closed the door of the closet and dialed the police. "There's an intruder in my house." He gave the address and said he would stay on the phone. The top step of the basement stairs creaked. Paley slowed her breathing and closed her eyes. She and Piedmont were sandwiched together. She huddled closer, pressing her face to his chest. His arm slid around her, his head rested on hers. His heart raced, or was that her heart? There was the soft shuffle of feet on carpet, the basement carpet, mere steps from the closet where they were hiding. Any minute the door would be opened and they would be discovered.

"The police have arrived," the dispatcher whispered.

The upstairs door opened again. "Lights on," Piedmont whispered. There was a frantic scrambling of feet, the grunting sounds of a physical struggle, and then the dispatcher spoke again.

"The suspect is in custody. The officers are going to sweep the house. One of them is heading toward your location. Please place your hands in the air as they open the door."

Piedmont and Paley complied, putting their hands up as the door was opened by a gun-wielding policeman. Paley had never been so happy to see anyone in her life, and she knew Piedmont felt the same. The intruder was on the ground, hands cuffed behind his back, but he was mere feet away. A few minutes later, and he would have found them.

"Are you okay?" the officer asked.

"Yes, thank you for arriving so quickly," Piedmont said.

"Ma'am?" the officer asked her. Paley tried to answer but no sound came out.

"Paley," Piedmont prompted, his hand rubbing a soothing circle on her back.

She jumped to attention and leaned into him at the same time. "Yes, I'm fine. And ditto what he said. Thank you so much for arriving so quickly."

The officer nodded and surveyed the suspect. "Either of you know him?"

They looked at the handcuffed man. "No," they both agreed.

"Probably a drug seeker," the officer said, but something in his tone worried them both. Or maybe they were so filled with fear everything sounded ominous. He wanted Piedmont to go with him to inspect the upstairs. Paley didn't want to be left alone. Sensing as much, Piedmont snagged her hand and dragged her with him.

"Nothing seems disturbed," they both agreed after an inspection of the house. "Nothing appears to have been taken."

The officer's frown increased. "We didn't find anything in his pockets."

"What does that mean?" Piedmont asked.

"Not for me to say, but I'll hand it over to our detective. Are you certain you locked the door?"

"Yes, I locked the door," Piedmont said.

"And I double checked that it was locked, I always do," Paley added.

"You do?" Piedmont asked.

"Sometimes you forget."

He tapped his temple and rolled his eyes. He was scatterbrained sometimes, but she had grown used to picking up the slack and making sure things got done. She squeezed his hand, offering up a smile.

"But you're both sure it was locked," the officer reiterated.

"Is there a reason you keep asking?"

"It doesn't appear to have been tampered with, and the alarm wasn't cut."

Paley shuddered. If he'd cut the alarm, she wouldn't have heard the beep, alerting her to the fact that the door had been opened. The man might have sneaked up on them unaware, and that was the disturbing thought she hadn't been able to pin down. "He was coming for us," she blurted.

Both men looked at her, Piedmont with surprise and the officer with affirmation. "He didn't pause to steal anything. If he was a drug seeker looking to make a quick buck, he would have loaded up and gotten out. He headed straight for the stairs, for us."

"It appears that way. Any reason?" Now the officer looked between them suspiciously.

"I deal with sensitive things occasionally. My last girlfriend was a target, she was kidnapped," Piedmont said, scowling. Was it happening again? Was Paley a target because of him? Or had he been the intended target this time?

"You're going to want to step up security," the officer said.

"I'll see what I can do. Should we go somewhere for the night?" Piedmont asked.

"No, I'll send a car around the neighborhood every so often, make sure anyone out there knows you're being watched. Unfortunately I can't do more than that, so you need to do something else from here on out."

"I will, thanks," Piedmont assured him.

They were still swarming the house, gathering evidence, writing reports, taking pictures. Paley made coffee and set out cookies from the freezer. Piedmont sat at the table and watched her. He wanted to ask her how she was doing, but she appeared to be trying to stay busy. The men gathered in the kitchen to partake of the treats, and then they were on their way. Without them, the house felt overwhelmingly large, dark, and scary.

Paley perched on the stool beside Piedmont. "Well, that was terrifying."

"Yep," Piedmont agreed.

"Goodnight then," she said, making no move to leave.

He laughed. "Heading off to the dark third floor alone, are you?"

"Mm, hmm. I'm brave."

"Okay, go on." He poked her.

"I couldn't possibly leave my employer here alone," she said. "Duty calls."

"We might as well find a place to stay up all night together because neither of us is going to sleep, possibly ever again," he said.

"I have a loveseat and a TV," she offered.

"Third floor is out, too remote and with no easy escape. Basement is out for the same reason," he said.

"Den couch is uncomfortable and not big enough for sprawling," she said.

"There's my bed, and I have a TV," he said.

She licked her lips. "It's too weird, isn't it?"

"We're grownups, we'll be fully clothed. Nothing's going to happen, just a little bit of human contact for comfort and reassurance," he said. "Plus you routinely handle my underwear. It's not like our boundaries are all that solid."

"Okay," she agreed. They stood, and she followed him to his room, pausing in the doorway to assess the large bed. "I don't know why this is weird. I lay in here every day eating crackers and watching TV while you're at work."

"So you're the source of the five pounds of cracker crumbs. I thought I was sleep eating again," he said. He crawled up onto the bed and reached for the remote. Paley walked around the bed and crawled up onto the other side. "What do you want to watch?"

"Your bedroom, your choice."

"Liar, you always have an opinion about things you think I need to see," he said.

"Let's watch baseball-themed movies."

"Am I supposed to pretend I know which those are, or are you going to tell me?" he said.

"Let's start with The Sandlot and work our way up to Field of Dreams," she suggested.

He found The Sandlot and set the remote on his nightstand. He glanced at Paley and saw her shivering. "Get under the covers."

She did so. A few minutes later when he looked at her again, she still shivered. "Are you doing that because you're still cold or as a delayed reaction to fear?"

"Neither. This is my Chihuahua imitation," she said.

He slid under the covers and reached for her. "You're safe, Paley."

"I know." She rested her head on his chest. "You're very good to have around in an emergency, quick thinking and lots of action. My first panicked thought was to run upstairs and save the knife block."

"Why?" he asked.

"Those are really nice knives," she said.

"My first thought was to save you," he said.

"I noticed. That's why I'm shivering now and not then because you made me feel safe, but now I'm thinking of all the ways it could have gone wrong," she said, shuddering anew.

"But it didn't. It's okay, everything is all right." His hand ran soothingly up and down her back. "Hey, look at me." She did so. "We're fine, we're safe, everything is good." He pushed the hair off her face. His hand slid to her cheek, cupping it, as his thumb slid over her lips. In the background, the movie blared.

"You're missing all the good stuff," she whispered.

"Pretty sure I'm not."

"Piedmont."

"Hmm." His thumb continued to slide over her lips, caressing them as he stared at them.

"We had a big, traumatic evening. It left me shivering and needy and you…whatever this is you are at the moment. Don't mistake it for something you'll regret tomorrow."

"I won't," he assured her, his hand not leaving her face.

"Don't mistake it for something I'll regret tomorrow." She said, and he froze. "I'm still married, by a thread and in name only, but still. It's not in my makeup to ignore that."

"I see," he said. He dropped his hand and eased away.

"Don't go away completely," she said, sounding pained.

"You want me to hold you and that's all?" he said.

"Can't that be enough?"

"For now," he said. She rested her head on his chest again. He eased his arms around her and ran a soothing hand over her hair. A few minutes later, she was asleep. Piedmont stayed awake to watch the entire movie. Eventually he, too, fell asleep, Paley still cradled in his clasp. When he woke the next morning, she was gone. He entered the kitchen and saw her making coffee and breakfast like usual. She set a mug and plate before him with a smile. Neither of them mentioned their close encounter again.

CHAPTER 18

"We want a pitcher, not a belly itcher; we want a catcher, not a belly scratcher."

"You're twelve," Mattie called in answer to Paley's song. "And you're the pitcher."

"He needs the full experience. That includes annoying, nonsensical songs," Paley called. She, her brother, Clark, Mattie, and a group of Clark's friends were showing Piedmont how to play baseball by forcing him to play a game of baseball.

"I've got it, I read all the books," Piedmont had assured Paley who responded by rolling her eyes.

"You can't learn how to play baseball by reading about it."

"I can quote every rule as well as all the statistics for the last ten years," he had said.

"Clearly you can learn, but those are only the technical aspects. You have to get the feel for the game," she had argued.

"I did that when you made me watch A League of Their Own. There's no crying in baseball. There, I'm all caught up on the feelings."

That was when she rested her hands on his shoulders and gave him what he now called her "chicken and waffles" look. Whenever she got it, he knew he was about to lose. "Piedmont, you're playing baseball."

It wasn't that he was averse to playing baseball. He was going to have to do it with the partners in his league, and it would be better to learn how to do it before an official game. It was that playing with her brother and Mattie and other friends made him nervous. They would undoubtedly judge him for his lack of knowledge on the sport. But Paley prevailed, and now he found himself in the outfield for his first ever inning of baseball. To his surprise, Paley pitched.

"She didn't tell you she played softball?" Mattie asked with a satisfied sort of grin that said he knew more about Paley than Piedmont ever would.

"We haven't been doing a lot of talking lately," Piedmont replied with a grin of his own. It was true; they'd resorted to a sort of half comfortable, half awkward silence since the night of the break in, the night of almost something.

Paley struck out the first three batters, and then it was Piedmont's turn at bat. "Mattie, show him how to bat," Paley called.

"Uh, no. You do it," Mattie replied, handing her the bat as he passed her and headed to her spot on the pitcher's mound.

"Like this," Paley said, placing the bat in his hands and reaching around him to position his hands and elbows. "Easy ones," she called to Mattie.

"This is so embarrassing," Piedmont said.

"It's all right. None of these guys would fare well going against you in court," she assured him. Mattie lobbed a slow ball at him. Piedmont swung and missed. "You're too tense, you're choking up." Paley reached around him again and corrected his stance. Mattie tossed another ball, and again Piedmont missed. "You're still tensing."

"I don't know how not to tense when something is flying at my face," he said.

She took the bat from him and held it. "Put your arms around me so you can see how it feels."

"I learned that the other night," he said.

"How it feels to hit the ball with the bat," she clarified.

"Oh, right," he said, sliding his arms around her.

"Feel the motion of your body as it swings, how it's sort of pivoting into it, it's a gentle sway, not a jerky, forced endeavor." She nodded at Mattie who tossed the ball again. She hit it, and Piedmont could feel the difference this time, vicariously through her. "Did that help?"

"Hopefully because this is getting pathetic."

"You're fine, everybody is here to help," she said, patting his back as she handed him the bat. Mattie tossed another ball. Piedmont hit it this time. It didn't go exceptionally far, but Paley yelled for him to run as if he'd hit a homer. She and Mattie traded places, and the game continued. Whether on purpose or whether the players on his team were better, he was able to make it to home plate and score a run. After that they got out and switched places again.

"Paley asked me to teach you how to catch," her brother, Clark, said. He was another surprise, tall, athletic, and good-looking, he had the innate confidence of a natural athlete. But like Paley he was nice, and there was none of the underlying tension he felt with Mattie. "Your glove needs to anticipate where the ball is going to land. Once the ball hits it, you bring it in to your body. Always protect your face." Clark lobbed him an easy toss from a few feet away, and Piedmont caught it. Clark tapped his glove, and Piedmont threw it back. It went wide, of course, but Clark dove and caught it before it hit the ground.

Piedmont sighed. He would never be that guy, the sure-footed athlete.

"Is it true you graduated high school at twelve?" Clark asked.

"Yes," Piedmont said. It was all he had, his genius intellect. Usually it was enough, but ever since Amelia married Ethan, he had noticed a glaring difference between himself and other men. And for the first time he found himself feeling insecure, wanting to be more than he was, wanting to be the guy who hit the home runs and caught the pop fly balls, who singlehandedly took down the bad guys and rescued the girl. What would he have done if the intruder had found them in the closet the other night? Would he have done everything in his power to protect Paley? And would it have been enough?

"Man, you graduated high school before you hit puberty, and you still turned out okay," Clark mused.

"Well, I'm learning to play baseball at the age of twenty seven, so I wouldn't say life's been perfect," Piedmont said.

"Lots of guys can't play ball. But you're the only one I know who's a genius," Clark said.

"Niceness must be in your blood," Piedmont noted. It was the kind of thing Paley would say to him.

"I know some women who would disagree," Clark said. They stood in the outfield and passed the ball a few times until Piedmont felt he had a better handle on catching. At least he was no longer afraid of the ball and knew how to protect his face. They switched to the dugout again, and all too soon it was his turn at bat.

Paley was still pitching. He took the bat and tried to remember to stand as she'd shown him. She motioned for him to raise it higher. He did so. She motioned again. He raised it higher. She motioned again. He raised it so high even he knew it was ridiculously out of place. She trotted over and hugged him, standing on her toes to whisper into his ear.

"Don't take direction from the pitcher. She's not on your team." She let him go, pulled his bat back into position, and jogged back to the mound.

"Was that necessary?" he called.

"You still feeling nervous?" she answered and tossed the ball before he had time to reply. Instinct seemed to take over, and he hit it farther than before and ran to his base without being told.

Mattie was at first base. "Rookie mistake, Bonvoy. Paley plays dirty."

"That's fine, so do I," Bonvoy replied and stole second.

Paley glanced at first, didn't see him, and turned in surprise to second. "Is that how you want to play?"

"That's how I want to play," he returned.

"Very well," she replied.

On his next turn at bat, he hit the ball, but Paley jumped and caught it. "That's an out," she called.

"I'm familiar with the rules," he returned.

"But not the feelings they inspire," she said.

He diverted from his trek to the dugout and ran out onto the mound instead, picking her up sideways and shaking her a few times for good measure.

"Roughing the pitcher," she said. "Foul. Penalty."

"None of those exist," he said. He set her down and kissed her forehead.

"If we win, we're all going to do that from now on," one of his teammates called. "For luck."

"You'll have to catch me, and I've seen you run, Bones," Paley replied.

"I like them feisty," Bones muttered.

Me too, Piedmont thought. He didn't realize this about himself until this moment, but he preferred women with zing and personality. Amelia'd had it, and so did Paley, though he felt like hers was buried beneath the layers of her painful divorce. He felt someone's eyes on him and turned to see Mattie watching him, an inscrutable expression on his face.

After the game was over, Mattie, Clark, and Piedmont were invited to Paley's parents' house for supper. Mattie and Clark were laughing and chatty, but Piedmont and Paley were quiet, subdued, each nervous for their own reasons. Paley knew exactly what to expect, but Piedmont didn't.

The house was like any other in the suburban Maryland neighborhood. Mattie was the one who opened the door for them, pausing in the entry to inhale the scent of homemade food.

"Mom, we're here," Clark called, following closely behind him.

A woman emerged from the kitchen and began giving hugs all around, first to Mattie, then to Clark, and finally to Paley. She stopped short in front of Piedmont, looking up at him in speculation. She was pleasant looking, like the sort of woman who smiled easily and said nice things often, slightly plump with glasses and curly dark hair like Clark's.

"Mom, this is my boss, Piedmont Bonvoy. Piedmont, this is my mother, Allison."

"Well, how do you do, Piedmont. It's so nice to meet you. Paley's told us a lot of wonderful things." She squinted. "Except how young and handsome you are." She tossed Paley an accusing glance.

"Subtle, Mom. Thanks for not making it awkward," Paley said, and Clark and Mattie laughed.

"Why don't you boys go call Dad and tell him supper's ready?" Allison suggested.

"Dad, supper's ready," Clark yelled at the top of his lungs, causing Allison to jump and cast a furious glance on her youngest.

"I said go tell him, not bellow like a heathen," Allison said.

"Do heathens bellow, Mom? I wouldn't know," Clark said, outlining a halo over his head.

Mattie snickered again. "I love it here."

"And we love having you," Allison said, reaching out to give his arm a loving pat. "Come on into the dining room now, everyone. Piedmont, please make yourself at home."

"Thank you," Piedmont said to her retreating backside. When Paley started to follow, he held her back. "She hates me."

"Of course she doesn't," Paley said.

Piedmont nodded.

"She really doesn't. She's disturbed because you're young. When I told her about you, I may have given her the impression you're old."

"Why?" he asked.

"Because I live with you, and I'm in the midst of a divorce she doesn't want to happen. She has ideas about things, and they rarely ever involve reality. She's now probably thinking you're standing between me and my reconciliation with Aaron."

"Doesn't she know about the baby?"

"It's hard to say. I told her, but what she allows to register and become reality in her world is impossible to guess," Paley said. She sighed and linked her arm with Piedmont's. "I did try to warn you they were different. Please believe me when I say it's not you, it's her. In time she'll grow to love you, I guarantee it."

"What can I do to speed the process along?"

"Nothing, you're totally lovable," she said, hugging him.

He returned her hug. "I'm going to bring you to your hometown more often if it has this effect on you. That's twice today you've hugged me."

"I suppose it does make me a tad more affectionate, being surrounded by familiar things and people."

"That settles it, we're moving in with your parents," he declared. Paley laughed and everyone paused to look at them as they walked into the dining room, still arm in arm.

"You sure about that plan?" she asked.

"Maybe hold off a bit," Piedmont replied, and Paley nodded her agreement.

CHAPTER 19

Though Paley had warned him about her family dynamic, Piedmont still found it fascinating. Her mother was willfully ignorant about factual information, and her father was fully in his own world, carrying on a conversation about grass with no one that lasted ten minutes. At last he asked Piedmont how he handled his grass. When Piedmont told him he had a lawn service, it was somehow another strike against him. He passed the remainder of the meal with his eyes narrowed on Piedmont, probably counting the silver, lest Piedmont attempt to swipe it and buy contraband weed controller.

Much to his surprise and appreciation, Mattie tried hard to carry the conversation and smooth things over. Undoubtedly this was for Paley's benefit, but Piedmont still appreciated it. It was obvious to anyone with eyes he cared deeply about her, but Piedmont still couldn't get a read on which way those feelings bent—true friendship or a desire for romance. Either way, he also seemed to hold Piedmont at arm's length and view him through a lens of deep suspicion. Did he think Piedmont was using Paley or playing with her heart? Something was off there, and Piedmont didn't know what.

Only Clark was open and friendly with no undercurrents, and Piedmont found himself gravitating to him, asking him questions whenever the conversation lagged. Clark was equally friendly and hadn't yet lost his fascination with Piedmont's genius status.

"So, what actually is your IQ?" he asked during one pause in the conversation.

"Clark, you can't ask that. It's like asking someone's pant size," Paley said.

"What's your pant size?" Clark asked her. "Because it looks smaller than I remember."

"Paley's lost weight," Mattie volunteered. "She's been working out."

"Why would you lose weight? Young girls always think they're heavy, but they're not. Everyone looks better with a little meat on the bones," Allison volunteered, adding a plop of mashed potatoes to Paley's plate.

"What is your IQ?" Paley's dad piped up. "If you don't mind saying."

"I don't mind saying, but it always feels a bit like bragging," Piedmont said.

"It's not bragging if they're asking for it," Paley said, a bit irritably. She rubbed at a spot between her eyebrows, a sure sign her family was getting to her. He could see why as her mother reached for the gravy and added it to Paley's potatoes uninvited.

"It's 210," Piedmont said.

"What? That's not possible. I thought the max was two hundred," Mattie said. He pulled out his phone and began to Google.

"It's not," Piedmont assured him. He tried to focus on his food, but his plate was empty, so he reached to Paley's plate and took some of her potatoes, causing Allison to frown and Paley to smile.

"Huh, he's right, it's not. It's rare though, like higher than Einstein rare," Mattie volunteered, shoving his phone back into his pocket.

Everyone gawked at Piedmont and Paley waved her hands. "Stop staring at him, he's not a circus freak."

Their eyes returned to their own plates, but conversation was on hold, and no one seemed to know how to get it started again.

"Have you heard from Aaron?" Allison asked.

"He tried, but I told him to talk to my lawyer."

Allison's hand settled onto the table with a thud. "You got a lawyer? Why?"

"Because I'm getting a divorce, Mom."

"You are? Since when?" Allison said.

"Since always. I told you Aaron kicked me out and started divorce proceedings," Paley said.

"That's a little blip." Allison picked up her fork and waved it dismissively. "You have to work at these things, Paley. Every marriage hits its bumps. If you gave up at every little fight, you'd never stay together. Your dad and I have had our rough patches, but we pulled together and persevered, and that's why we're so happy today." She cast a glance to her husband who stared at his pot roast, oblivious to his wife's words. She sighed and turned back to Paley. "I think you should meet with Aaron in person. A lot can be communicated face to face."

"I don't want Paley to do that," Piedmont said, and now everyone turned to look at him in surprise.

"I don't see that it's any of your business," Allison said.

"Mom," Paley intoned.

"I do," Piedmont said.

"And why do you feel it's your right to tell her not to meet with her husband?" Allison demanded.

"Because I'm a lawyer, and I know how divorce proceedings go. He's trying to take advantage of her, to get her to give up everything in the settlement, to leave her with nothing."

"If she talked to him, there might not be a divorce," Allison said.

"Mom," Paley tried, but Piedmont put his hand on hers.

"Allison, do you believe it takes two people to make a marriage work?" Piedmont asked.

"Yes, but…"

"Knowing Paley as you do, do you think she gave it her all as a wife, that she was loyal, faithful, loving, hard working?"

"Yes, but…"

"Do you believe your daughter deserves the same loyalty, faithfulness, kindness, and hard work from a spouse?"

"Yes, but…"

"Do you honestly believe Aaron gave her that? That he was kind to her, supportive, said nice things, treated her the way you would wish for her to be treated?"

"No, but…"

"If you believe he didn't treat her the way she should be treated, if you believe Paley tried hard at her marriage and he didn't, don't you believe sentencing her to remain with someone who doesn't love her, with someone who cheated on her and impregnated another woman, would be tantamount to abuse?"

"I…I don't…" Allison floundered.

"We all want what's best for Paley, don't we?" Piedmont pressed.

Allison nodded, out of words now.

"And we all trust that Paley is capable of figuring out what that is, don't we?"

Allison nodded again.

"Good, we agree," Piedmont said and scraped all of Paley's potatoes onto his plate.

"Case closed," Mattie said, and Clark snickered into his napkin.

After that, somehow things were better. The argument, if it could be called such, had cleared the way for Paley's parents' approval somehow. In any case they were less suspicious of him, more trusting, more eager to like him. Her dad even walked him outside and showed him the grass.

"I've tried everything, but it's still brown," he said in dismay.

"Dad, Piedmont doesn't…" Paley began, but Piedmont held up a hand, bent, and inspected the grass, running his hand softly over the top of it.

"Your lawnmower blades are dull. It's tearing the grass. And you're watering too much. Water every other day, sharpen your blades, and raise the height of you mower deck," Piedmont said.

"Tearing the grass," her father said, kneeling to inspect the torn blades before him. "By gum, I think you're right."

"How did you possibly know that?" Paley asked, leading him back inside while her father remained kneeling beside the grass. It was possible he was apologizing to it. She tried never to peer too closely into her father's odd relationship with the lawn.

"I researched grass on the off chance it would come up," Piedmont said.

"That might be the sweetest, most adorable thing I've ever heard," Paley said.

"Clearly you need to get out more, if that's the case," he said.

"Did you research anything for my mom?" she asked.

"Nope," he said, but he wouldn't make eye contact.

"What?" she asked, poking him.

"I researched how to impress your girlfriend's mother," he said, his tone sheepish.

"Huh. It's lucky that also applied to meeting your housekeeper's mother," she said.

"It's a startling coincidence how much and how often the two intersect and overlap these days," he said. He took her hand and pulled her close, snugging her against his chest. "There's one glaring difference, however."

"What?" she whispered.

He leaned down to whisper in her ear. "My housekeepers and I always spend a lot of time making out. It's usually a highly physical relationship."

"It's not like that between us," she said.

"Then I guess that shifts you into the other category," he said, squeezing her hand.

She blinked at him, a bit stunned. Was he saying...?

"Let's play two on two," Clark said, palming a basketball as he entered the room, followed by Mattie.

"Yes," Paley replied, her eyes still on Piedmont.

"Yes to..." he drawled.

"What do you think? I'm a sucker for basketball," she said, stealing the ball from her brother and tossing it to Piedmont who somehow caught it.

"It goes without saying I only know the technical aspects of basketball," he said.

"Then it's time you got all the feelings," Paley said and, taking his hand, led him outside.

CHAPTER 20

The drive home was silent, almost expectant. Piedmont drove, knowing instinctively it would not have gone over well if he'd shown up with a driver. He hadn't driven in a while and was a little out of touch with the practicalities. He told himself that was why he didn't talk to Paley on the way home, but it wasn't true. The truth was that he was confused and a little bit concerned.

Their relationship was shifting. Did he want it to? Was he ready for that? Was she? The answer to that was a definite no. She had made it clear nothing could happen between them until her divorce was official. Her husband, who had initiated the process, was now dragging his heels, slowing it down and making it take forever, probably to punish her for his assumption that she and Piedmont were together. Even though he was with someone who was carrying his baby, someone he presumably wanted to marry, he would make the divorce take forever to cause Paley pain and aggravation. A prince among men was her ex.

And then there was the fact that she was his housekeeper. If they became more than that, could he keep paying her to work for him? That felt weird, but she was also the best housekeeper he'd had, and he didn't want to lose that. Was it a sign of his own selfishness that he worried who would take care of him if Paley left his employment? Yes, but he couldn't seem to help it. He hated the thought of breaking someone else in, of having someone else in his space. And she was good at it, excellent at arranging his life without being obvious about it. Like Acacia at work, she seemed to have a sixth sense about what he needed, often before he realized he needed it.

Thankfully the inertia imposed by her impending divorce bought them some time. He was certain they could come to a workable solution. In the meantime, he merely had to fend off his own temptation where she was concerned.

He caught a glimpse of her, her hair in a cute ponytail, her t-shirt still covered in dust from baseball. "You didn't tell me you were sporty." He poked her.

"I thought it was assumed," she said, poking him in return.

"Why would it be assumed?" he asked, poking her again.

"Because I wear t-shirts and hoodies all the time and enjoy manual labor," she said, poking him.

His mouth opened in a pucker of surprise. "You're right, I should have figured that out." She gave him a smile. "Stop lording it over me when I don't know things. I'm not omniscient."

"Nearly. 210. Geez."

"Don't be intimidated by me now because you know the number," he said.

"Last week I saw you miss the bottom step because you were reading while walking down the stairs. I think we're safe," she said.

"I did that on purpose; it was an experiment," he said.

"To test the strength of the banister you grabbed?" she asked.

"Exactly. Thanks for sticking around to make sure I was okay."

"I couldn't, I was laughing too hard," she said.

"I know, I heard you all the way in the kitchen," he said. "It's about time for me to fire you again."

"Let another woman touch my knives, and I'll cut you," she warned.

Her tone was joking, but he wondered if she was having similar thoughts to his about their precarious position and a possible replacement for her. "No one's touching your knives," he assured her, reaching out to clasp her hand.

She stared out the window, not answering. He both wanted to know and didn't want to know what she thought. They pulled into the driveway, and she turned to face him, smiling. "Thanks for today. It was fun."

"You're the one who arranged it," he said.

"You know what I mean. You went over and above with my family, and I appreciate it. A lot. It's possible you got my mom to actually understand the impossible situation with Aaron, and that means more than you could know." She leaned over the divider and kissed his cheek. She would have pulled away, but his hand reached out, holding her back.

"Paley," he whispered. She froze, hovering uncomfortably over the divider, when a new car pulled in behind them. Paley tensed, and so did he, but for vastly different reasons. Paley didn't know who the newcomer was, but Piedmont did. They stepped out of the car at the same time as the new arrival. He was tall and well dressed, but Paley somehow thought the suit was an odd fit for him. He seemed like the kind of guy who would be more comfortable in a uniform, possibly a cop or soldier.

"Piedmont," he said, extending his hand to shake.

"Cameron," Piedmont replied, returning the shake. "This is Paley. Paley, this is Amelia's brother-in-law, Cameron Ridge."

"How do you do," Cameron said, extending his hand to Paley. She shook it with a wary smile. Was he there to tell on her, to warn her away from ever contacting Amelia again? Piedmont still didn't know about her subversive salon visit. If he did, he'd likely feel angry, possibly betrayed. She thought she caught a twinkle of amusement in Cameron's eyes, and she wondered if he knew what she thought. "Can I talk to you?" he asked Piedmont. In private was both unspoken and implied.

"I'll make coffee and set out some cookies," Paley volunteered, lightly touching Piedmont's arm before disappearing inside the house.

"Congratulations, I didn't know you were with someone,"

Cameron said.

"She's...I'm...thanks," Piedmont said. "Come inside." He led the way to the living room and sat down, Cameron following suit on the opposing couch. "How's Maggie?"

"She's well, thanks. I'm sure you're wondering why I'm here."

Piedmont decided to be honest. At one point he thought this man would be his brother-in-law, and he wasn't exactly thrilled by the reminder that he wasn't. "Yes."

"A detective called me about your recent break in. He knew my family's connection to you and wanted to give me a heads up."

Piedmont's stomach pitched and dropped. There could only be one reason for that, and it wasn't good. "Go on," he croaked.

"It was a professional hit, but thankfully he was intercepted before he got the job done. The equipment was sophisticated, and the guy has a suspected history of confirmed kills a mile long."

"The Russians again?" Had it been retaliation for saving Amelia, whom they'd kidnapped a few months ago?

"No, there, uh, aren't enough of them left alive to carry out such a venture," Cameron said.

Piedmont winced. He knew the likelihood that Ethan had killed one or more of Amelia's captors, but the certainty hadn't been confirmed until now. "Who is it then?"

"We don't know. I had my team go over everything and everyone you're currently working on, and everyone is clean. That leads me to believe it's some kind of retaliation for a former case. Any ideas?"

Piedmont wracked his brain. He'd won a lot of cases, made a lot of enemies. None of them had obvious ties to the mob, at least none he knew of. "No one comes to mind, but I'll keep thinking about it."

"Good, keep me informed. We'll keep digging, too. I'll let you know if we come up with anything."

Paley made a timely return before the conversation dwindled to awkwardness. She served coffee and cookies and would have removed herself again, but Piedmont held her back.

"These cookies are amazing. My wife would flip," Cameron noted. "She's something of a cookie connoisseur."

"Paley makes the best desserts I've ever tasted," Piedmont said, resting his hand on her knee with a smile that looked a bit melancholy. Paley raised her eyes in question. He shook his head.

"I'll send some for your wife," Paley volunteered, ripping her eyes from Piedmont to focus on Cameron Ridge. Like Amelia's husband, he was an intensely handsome man, the kind who exuded raw testosterone and protective manly instincts. The kind of man, she knew, who made Piedmont feel insecure, Piedmont with his kindness, care, compassion, and ridiculous intelligence. A man who'd achieved more in his short life than most people in a lifetime felt somehow less because he couldn't throw a punch as well as the man now sitting before them. She rested her hand on Piedmont's leg and gave it a reassuring squeeze. If she had the choice between an Ethan, a Cameron, and a Piedmont, she would always choose Piedmont with the gentle eyes and sweet smile, the goofy sense of humor and genius IQ.

She disappeared to the kitchen and returned a minute later with a plate of wrapped cookies for Cameron to take home to his wife.

"Don't be surprised if she calls you and asks for more," Cameron warned.

"Anytime," Paley said and meant it. She had nothing against this man or his wife, and she knew Piedmont didn't either, regardless of the bad breakup looming between them.

"Thank you," Cameron said. "Piedmont, keep me informed, and I'll do the same."

"Absolutely," Piedmont agreed, shaking hands again. He and Paley stood at the door together and saw Cameron out, his arm resting on her shoulder as if they were lord and lady of the manor together instead of employer and housekeeper. Long after Cameron was gone, Piedmont remained staring dully through the door. He'd done it again. Somehow his job had put someone he cared about in danger. How did it happen, and how could he stand it?

"Piedmont," Paley said at last, placing a feather soft hand on his side.

He jumped nonetheless and looked at her. "I think you should move back in with your parents for a while."

CHAPTER 21

In the end, Piedmont lost the argument. Paley assumed her chicken-and-waffles expression and no amount of persuasion on his part would sway her, which was doubly infuriating since rhetorical persuasion was kind of what he was known for. Why was he able to influence a jury of twelve people with the power of his words, but not this one person he paid to do what he said? It was maddening.

As a compromise to Paley remaining in the house, he bought them each a gun and they took shooting lessons together.

"I'm exhausted," Paley said as they sat side by side on the couch after their first day of shooting.

"But you look cute, and that's what's important," Piedmont said, his tone slightly bitter.

"You have to let it go," Paley said.

"I'm paying the guy to teach you to shoot, not to flirt with you," Piedmont said.

"How do you know he was flirting? Maybe he's merely friendly," she suggested.

"Oh, please," he said. "Although he did have a point, you do look cute. Do you know what I want to do now?" He reached for her and pulled her into his lap.

"What?"

"That was it, I just did it. Your turn to think of something."

"This will do for now," she said. The last few days they had been hovering in between something yet undefined by either of them. "Are you going to buy a safe like the guy suggested?"

"I don't think so because we'll always have our guns on us, which is kind of the point of getting them and learning to use them. A safe is for when there are small children around. Someday I suppose I'll have to get a safe, if I keep the gun."

"Oh, right," she said, suddenly withdrawing into herself and turning pensive.

"What?" he asked.

"Nothing."

"What?" he asked, squeezing her thigh.

"I was imagining your future children," she said.

"And that depresses you why?" he asked.

"Because I'm unable to imagine where I fit in the scenario," she said. "Will they come visit Weird Aunt Paley, the upstairs maid?"

"Paley, come on," he said.

"Come on what?" she said.

"You really don't know where you fit in that scenario?" he asked.

She shook her head.

"Would you like me to tell you?"

She nodded, heart thumping. He took her hands in his, and the doorbell rang. With a sigh, he picked up his phone and looked at it, checking the video monitor. "It's for you." He held it out to her, showing Aaron on the screen.

She sighed in the same fashion and took the phone, pushing the button to activate the speaker on the front porch. "What do you want, Aaron?"

Aaron frowned. "You really are living here. I didn't believe it. Wow, okay."

"Was that all you wanted? To confirm my address?" she asked.

"No, I want to talk to you."

"Go ahead, I'm listening."

"Face to face, Paley."

"I can see your face," she said. It was still stupidly handsome. Had she been so easily duped by his good looks, or had he laid on the charm so thick she hadn't seen through it? The thought still bothered her. Where had she gone wrong in her selection of him?

"But I can't see yours."

"It still looks the same," she assured him.

"No, it doesn't. You got some kind of makeover, and you look… good. You look really pretty, Paley."

"Thank you."

"This is fun, thanks for making me a part of it," Piedmont whispered. She pressed her palm to his mouth, and he kissed it.

"That's it? That's all you have to say?"

"Aaron, please get to the point. What do you want?" Paley asked.

"I want you to back your lawyer off the assets. I'm going to have to sell the house."

Piedmont shook his head and whispered, "Equitable distribution."

"I'm not taking more than my share; it's equitable distribution," Paley said.

"I know, Paley, I went to law school. But I'm not going to have anywhere to live, Melinda's not going to have anywhere to live, and the baby's due soon."

Paley held the phone away from her and spoke to Piedmont. "Am I hearing him right? Is he trying to make me feel bad that his pregnant mistress isn't going to be able to sleep in my bed at night?"

"How can you be so heartless?" Piedmont said. "Next you'll try to make him believe she's his responsibility and not yours. The woman is having your husband's baby. How can you be so cruel?"

Paley rolled her eyes and shook her head, putting the phone back to her face. "Really, Aaron, really?"

"You never even liked the house," he said.

"All the more reason to sell it and split the proceeds," she said. "You and your…friend can buy something of your own together."

"We can't afford that," he spat.

"Just like we couldn't afford the house we bought. I tried to tell you from the beginning it was too much debt. You can rent for a while."

Piedmont shook his head. "Stop trying to solve his problems. He's a grown man, presumably," he whispered.

"I know, but old habits die hard," Paley whispered.

"While you live here, shacking up in luxury with your new boyfriend."

Piedmont nodded, smiling now.

"Did you purposely go for him because you knew it would hurt me? I bet you couldn't wait, I bet you had your sights set on him from the beginning. When did it start? How long have you been together? Because you're already living with him, and there's no way you move that quickly, which makes me think it must have started before. Were you seeing him behind my back while we were together?" Aaron demanded.

Paley didn't answer because she was too busy trotting to keep up with Piedmont as he steamrolled toward the front door. He yanked it open and Aaron blinked at him in surprise, clearly not expecting to see him, even though it was his house.

"You're going to have to leave now," Piedmont said.

"I want to talk to Paley," Aaron insisted.

"You already did. Anything else you have to say can be said to her lawyer."

"The lawyer you're paying for, you mean. There's no way Paley can afford him," Aaron said.

"Not your business," Piedmont said.

"She's my wife," Aaron argued.

"Not for much longer," Piedmont replied. "And before you say anything else, I'd like to caution you that you're coming scarily close to slander, something I and my reputation take extremely seriously."

"I tried to do this the nice way, but if you want a fight, you've got it. And I'm going to win," Aaron declared.

"Don't you understand? You sent Paley away; you've already lost," Piedmont said.

Aaron turned and stalked away. Piedmont softly closed the door. "How are you holding up?" he asked Paley.

"I'm fine, it's just…"

"Just what?" he asked.

"I feel like you're always rescuing me," she said.

"You do?" he asked in surprise. He didn't feel that way. He wasn't doing anything out of the norm, merely being himself.

She nodded. He opened his arms, and she stumbled into them, snuggling close against his chest. His hand smoothed up and down her spine, and she shivered. "Until this is resolved, I can't…" she began.

"I know," he interrupted her. "That doesn't stop us from being friends."

"You're my favorite," she said.

"Ditto," he agreed, giving her a squeeze.

CHAPTER 22

A few days later, Piedmont called Paley from work.

"What are you wearing?" he started the conversation.

"You even have to ask?" she replied.

"TARDIS costume?" he guessed.

"Was there any question?" she countered.

"This is so awkward, that's exactly what I'm wearing, too. Bosses are not happy," he said.

"It's going to make for some awesome court pictures," she said. "How's your day, really?"

"Good. Yours? All quiet?" They'd been on edge since the home invasion, but so far nothing had happened.

"All is well," she assured him. "What's up?"

"Can't a guy call to chat?" he said.

"Yes, but you don't generally call without a purpose," she said.

"Today is no different. I'm going to be home at six tonight," he said.

"Why so early?" he usually got home much later. In the beginning, she had left a meal for him. At some point that changed and she began waiting to dine with him.

"I felt like having an evening with my girl," he said.

"Do I know her?" Paley replied.

"You're full of sass today," he said. "Might be time to fire you again."

"Go ahead because I got an order for a hundred cookies, so clearly I can make it on my own and my overt reliance on you is an illusion," she said.

"I've been dreading the day you'd come to that realization," he said. "Who are the cookies for?"

She paused. "Maggie Ridge. Is that okay?"

"Yes, I like Maggie, and I like you, so it's a win-win."

"You're cute."

"How do you know? You haven't seen me since this morning. I might have aged ugly," he said.

"Your cuteness is innate," she said. "Any requests for supper?"

"Something edible."

She huffed. "Control freak much?"

"Incessantly, all the time. See you at six."

"See you," Paley said. Despite his words to the contrary, she had the sense there was something special in his early arrival from work. For that reason, she put more than usual into her performance, going so far as to change into a skirt and dry and style her hair, a switch from her usual jeans and ponytail.

He arrived home with flowers. "Seriously, what is up?" Paley said, reaching for a vase.

"Nothing," he said, but his secret smile said otherwise.

"You're making me suspicious because I can tell you're keeping secrets. Are you divorcing me, too?"

"Can't a guy bring his housekeeper flowers and not have it be weird?" he asked.

"I'm beginning to see why the others left. Or did they leave? Am I eventually going to find them tied up in the house somewhere?" she asked.

"So suspicious," he said. "What can I do to help with supper?"

"Eat it," she suggested.

"Now who's a control freak," he countered. He started to sit at the kitchen island, but she stopped him.

"We're eating in the dining room tonight," she said.

"Really? That's fancy," he said.

"Call me crazy, but it feels like a special occasion," she said.

"Crazy," he said, but he smiled the smile again. He helped her carry dishes into the dining room, and they sat down to eat. He kept the conversation light and casual over supper, but that only increased Paley's suspense. She knew he held out on her, and she began to realize it was something big. But every time she asked what it was, he changed the topic to something else, dodging the question entirely.

Finally after supper was over and dessert was finished, he set down his coffee and faced her. Paley's heart began to beat hard with anticipation. "I wonder," he said.

"Yes?" she said.

"What's left on my list?"

"List, what list?" She squinted. Had he left a list of things for her to do and she somehow forgot?

"My list of things I missed out on for being an oddball child prodigy," he said.

"Oh, I'd have to look, but we're getting down to the dregs. I remember ice skating, camping in a tent, and Capture the Flag. I'd have to check it to see what else."

His finger rimmed the coffee cup in front of him. "Was there anything about making partner on that list?"

She froze. Was he saying what she thought he was saying? "Piedmont, don't toy with me. Are you being serious?"

He nodded. "I made partner."

She launched herself at him, and he caught her. "This is…I don't think I've ever been this happy or excited in my life. Congratulations, you deserve this so much. All your hard work, and, oh my goodness, I'm out of words." She hugged him tightly, crying more than a little.

"Thank you," he said, holding her close.

"You must be the youngest person in their history to ever make partner," she said.

"I am," he agreed.

She squeezed him tighter. "I'm so proud of you. I can't believe this, it's amazing."

"I've been dying to tell you, holding it in for six hours."

"The suspense was killing me," she said.

"Me, too," he agreed. He pushed away from the table and pulled her into his lap. "There's more. The partners want to take us out to celebrate. Tomorrow."

She froze. "Tomorrow?"

"Yes, I know you have the thing with Mattie, but I thought maybe you could reschedule," he said.

"I can't," she whispered. "I can't reschedule. That's why I told you about it a month in advance, so there would be no conflict. I need to spend tomorrow night with Mattie."

"Paley, this is important to me, it's once in a lifetime," he said.

"Piedmont, I know, and it's killing me, but I gave Mattie my word. I have a prior commitment. Is there a chance of changing your celebration to any other day?"

"No. I didn't choose the date, the partners did. I can't go to them and say I can't make it because you have another date."

She let out a breath.

"Paley."

She shook her head slowly, sadly. "I can't. I can't change it."

"I guess you've made your decision then," he said.

"Don't say it like that."

"Like what?"

"Like you're making it a choice between you and Mattie," she said.

"I'm not, you are. And apparently you already chose." He stood up, easing away from her. "Excuse me, I have some things to see to." He left the room.

Paley cleaned the kitchen and retired to her room. All night long she expected Piedmont to show up and talk things through. He never did, and she made no move to seek him out, either.

CHAPTER 23

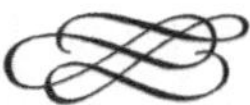

The next morning Piedmont was having thoughts. He expected to come upstairs from his workout, find Paley waiting with a smile, ready to make up. But there was no Paley. His coffee and muffins were there, along with his sack lunch, but she was nowhere to be found. He grabbed the coffee and muffin, left the lunch, and went to his room to get ready. She didn't say goodbye when he left, nor hug him, as had become her custom the last couple of weeks as their relationship hung in the balance between friendship and something more.

Piedmont was furious and trying not to show it, but of course Acacia realized. And when one of the partners asked if Paley was excited for the upcoming dinner, he had to tell the truth—she had a prior engagement and couldn't make it.

"Oh, we'll make it next week. Would that work?" Arthur asked.

Piedmont blinked at him, feeling like a fool for blowing things so out of proportion. "Yes, that works perfectly, thank you."

After that he tried to call Paley, but she didn't answer. When he arrived home, she was already gone for her evening with Mattie, and Piedmont was irritated all over again. She had been cryptic about the night out with Mattie, and he couldn't tamp down a vague uneasy feeling. There was something Paley wasn't telling him, and it harkened him back to conversations with Amelia about Ethan. You talk about Ethan a lot, he had said. He's a friend, Amelia insisted. A friend like Mattie was a friend to Paley? Was he doomed to fall for women who fell for their male best friends?

She didn't arrive home until late. Piedmont sat on the couch in the basement, trying to figure out what to watch without her there to tell him. Under her direction he had watched a lot of movies he missed out on during his unusual upbringing, and now suddenly a lot of pop culture references he'd never understood made sense. But without her he had no idea how to continue or what to watch. He ended up watching baseball and trying to pretend he found it interesting, but really it reminded him of Paley and the day she'd taught him to bat.

The door opened and closed, alerting him to the fact she'd arrived home. Footsteps echoed on the stairs, and he braced himself for the coming conversation. He needed to apologize, but he was still hurt, his pride still wounded.

When the couch beside him shifted, it wasn't Paley; it was Mattie.

"You're watching baseball. I didn't see that coming," Mattie remarked.

"It's like watching paint dry. I'm in misery," Piedmont admitted. He turned the TV off and dropped the remote.

"You think I'm jealous of you, and you're jealous of me," Mattie said. Piedmont didn't deny it. "Both things are either untrue or unnecessary."

"I hope there's a follow up to explain," Piedmont said.

"There is. Paley and I have been friends forever, since she first moved here when we were prepubescent. What you don't know is we weren't always a duo—we were a trio. Jenny was our counterpoint, the solidifying member of our group. When we were freshmen, Jenny and I shifted naturally into a dating relationship. It was one of those things where even though we were young, we knew we'd be together forever. And Paley wasn't a third wheel, it was still the three of us against the world, but the dynamics shifted slightly.

"Our senior year, I had to work one night and the two of them went out without me. Jenny was driving, and a sudden storm sprang up, the kind with wind and a downpour that drops visibility to zero. They hydroplaned and hit a tree. Paley was unhurt, thankfully, but Jenny was killed on impact. The tree fell on the car, trapping them inside. Neither of them had their phones. They weren't found until two hours later when I realized I hadn't heard from them and alerted their parents. Everyone went out to look for them. Paley sat there all that time, holding Jenny's lifeless, cold hand, talking to her, begging her to hang on, to come back.

"We were there for each other in our grief. A few months later, I kissed her, and she kissed me back. We dated for about a month and tried to convince ourselves it was real before calling it quits. We both loved Jenny too much to fake it any longer. I still love Jenny. I always will. Paley and I are friends, but nothing beyond that. It fizzles impossibly, it always has, and it always will.

"You have to understand Paley was our sparkle, our sunshine. Jenny was the reserved, steady one of our group. Everyone liked Paley. She was our homecoming queen, played every sport, was nice to everyone. But after that night...she faded, like someone closing the blinds on the sun. Then she married the jerk, and he tried to tamp down whatever bit of spirit was left in her.

"The last few months I've seen her start to come back, to find some of that old sparkle and sunshine, and I guess I do guard it rather jealously, but only because I'm afraid it's going to go away again. I don't know you or your intentions toward her. You're rich and successful, and she's your maid, never a good combination. Mostly, I don't want to see her hurt again, to see the girl I know disappear again."

"What was significant about tonight?" Piedmont asked.

"The accident was ten years ago tonight. It's always a hard night for both of us. I asked Paley to spend it with me, knowing we'd both need the comfort and commiseration."

"I don't think I could feel like any more of a selfish heel," Piedmont said.

"Probably if I told you she's upstairs weeping right now," Mattie said.

Piedmont groaned. "I should go to her."

"She doesn't know I'm here, and she'd be mortified if you caught her crying. For both our sakes, you should wait," Mattie said. "But it sounds like it was an important night for you, too. It killed her not to be there with you, but that's who Paley is. She's loyal and she keeps her word."

"I know," Piedmont said.

"Congratulations, by the way," Mattie said.

"Thank you." He picked up the remote. "Do you want to watch baseball?"

"Less than anything. Let's watch The Princess Bride."

"Paley makes me watch that one approximately once a week," Piedmont said.

"That's what makes her good people," Mattie said. He sank lower onto the couch, and they settled in to watch the movie.

The next morning, Paley still didn't show for breakfast. Piedmont contemplated going to get her, but figured he would let her have some more time to cool down. Tonight they would work everything out. Best of all, he would be able to tell her she hadn't missed the partner's dinner, that it was a go for next week. She had set out his coffee, breakfast, and lunch like usual, and he took the lunch this time.

Paley emerged from her room after he was gone, feeling like a coward. She and Piedmont needed to make up soon, but she couldn't face his anger or hurt today. She knew he must feel both because she had missed his big dinner, and she felt horrible about that. Last night had been emotionally draining on its own with Mattie, disregarding any tension with Piedmont. She couldn't handle both things right now. Later, she was certain they would clear the air. Or so she hoped.

With that thought in mind, she threw herself into cleaning with a vengeance, tackling everything she had been putting off. She was upstairs when the doorbell rang. She reached for her phone, pushed the button, and saw two men standing on the porch, both wearing suits.

"May I help you?"

"Federal marshals, ma'am, we'd like to talk to you."

Paley almost ran down the stairs and let them in, but a little warning voice held her back. Instead she called Piedmont, forgetting he was in court. His phone forwarded to Acacia.

"There are two men on the front porch who say they're federal marshals," Paley said.

"And you don't think they are?" Acacia said.

"I don't know, but Piedmont asked me to be extra careful and wary. I'm not sure how to check if they're legit or not," Paley said.

"I'll call the Marshal's office," Acacia said. "Hold on."

"Okay, I'll give them an excuse to stall," Paley said. She pushed the button and spoke to the men. "Give me a second, please, I'm just getting out of the shower." There was no answer. Frowning, she switched to the video monitor on the phone, but the porch was empty. She flipped back to Acacia. "I think it's okay, they appear to be go…" She froze as the sound of a gun being cocked registered from behind her.

"Paley, what's going on, what happened?" Acacia asked, but the next thing she heard was an ear-shattering gunshot.

CHAPTER 24

Piedmont knew it was serious when he was summoned from court. Acacia had never done that before, not once. Only the direst circumstance would provoke such an action. He was prepared for the worst, or so he thought. When he learned about the phone call and the gunshot, it was so much worse than he'd imagined.

He couldn't think clearly—only one thing made sense. He gave Charles directions and headed to the only place that came to mind.

When Amelia answered the door and saw her ex-boyfriend on the other side, she blinked at him in surprised confusion, speechless. "I need you," Piedmont declared.

"Um," Amelia said, unsure how to respond.

He peered around her, to the other person in the apartment. "Not you, sorry. Ethan, I need you."

Ethan came to the door and stood beside Amelia. "What's the problem?"

"They took Paley, and she might be shot."

Amelia gasped. Ethan nodded, reached behind the door and grabbed a black bag. "I'm ready."

"You're already ready to go?" Piedmont said.

"Not my first time," Ethan said. He kissed Amelia goodbye, closed the door, and they were on their way. "Tell me everything you know."

So Piedmont filled him in on the home invasion as well as the mob connection and his inability to determine who ordered the first hit. They reached Charles, and Ethan waved him away. "We'll take my car, at this point I don't trust anyone who's not on my team. Call the detective handling the case and have him send you a picture of the room she was taken from, the one with the blood."

Piedmont did as he was instructed. A minute later, he had the picture on his phone. They came to a red light, and Ethan studied it. "Does she have a gun?"

"Yes, we've been taking lessons," Piedmont said.

Ethan tipped his head. "It's likely she was by the bed and the intruders entered the room, meaning she was the shooter and one of them is injured. Judging by the amount of blood, it wasn't a fatal shot." He handed the phone back to Piedmont who studied it, trying to figure out what he saw that gave him that idea. Was he merely trying to make Piedmont feel better? But no, Ethan wasn't the kind to sugar-coat things. Paley had likely been in the midst of cleaning. The bed was half made, meaning she was in the middle of making it. She had probably heard the intruders, spun, and fired her weapon. He smiled a little, proud of her spunk in the face of certain terror. He could only hope it hadn't enraged her captors, hadn't prompted them to retaliate.

They pulled into the parking garage of a high-rise building downtown.

"What are we doing here?" Piedmont asked.

"Getting some much needed help," Ethan said. He pushed a button.

"What?" a voice said.

"It's me," Ethan said.

The voice sighed, but soon the elevator doors opened, and they were granted access to the top floor, the penthouse.

The door was opened by someone Piedmont knew, a friend of Amelia's named Blue. He'd always felt a certain affinity with Blue, recognition from one geek to another. He had no idea what Blue's connection to Ethan was, but he figured it must be something to do with his job, that Blue functioned in a secret capacity that had been kept hidden.

"I just got home, Becket," Blue complained.

"It's not for me, it's for him," Ethan said, thumbing in the direction of Piedmont.

Blue sighed. "Him I like. Come on in. How's it going, Piedmont?"

"Not so well."

"His girlfriend was kidnapped," Ethan explained.

Blue looked at him, frowning. "You do have a way with the ladies."

Piedmont glanced at Ethan in question. "Blue's the one who located Amelia for us last time."

Piedmont blinked at Blue in surprise and then, for lack of anything better to do, stared around the spacious abode. "I think I used to own this building," he noted absently. He had an investment portfolio, and real estate was part of it. He only paid vague attention to the things his broker bought and sold for him, but he'd always liked the building in question.

"You did." A small woman on the couch piped up. She sat absolutely still, so still and silent Piedmont didn't notice her until she spoke. In her lap was a massive volume with a picture of a mummy on the cover. "Piedmont Bonvoy," she said in acknowledgement of his inspection before returning her attention to her book.

"How could you possibly know that?" Blue asked.

"I snooped through your financial records," she said, not bothering to look up again.

"For that, I'm making you a Facebook account when I'm done with this," Blue threatened.

"My dad will be thrilled," Jane said, and Ethan snickered.

"This was worth the price of admission," he said. "But not really," he added, catching sight of Piedmont's frown.

"Here we go," Blue said, and the three men leaned forward in time to watch a grainy video of Paley being stuffed into the back of a car. "Got a plate."

He typed some more while Piedmont's insides twisted with anxiety. She had been alive when she was put into the car. If they wanted to kill her, they could have done it immediately at the house. It had to be some kind of ransom situation. He hoped so, or why else would they have a need to hold onto her?

"Here we go," Blue repeated, and everyone froze again. The car stopped in front of another house.

"That's Paley's former house," Piedmont said. They watched as another woman was gathered and stuffed into the back of the car, this one obviously pregnant.

"You know her?" Ethan asked.

"That's Paley's husband's girlfriend," Piedmont said. "What would they want with her?"

"Let's see," Blue said, and began typing again.

"Paley Anderson?" the woman on the couch asked. Piedmont turned to her in surprise.

"You know Paley?"

"She and my younger sister, Poppy, are 4H frenemies."

"What are 4H frenemies?" Ethan asked, plopping down beside her and helping himself to a bowl of candy on the table.

"They had a mutual interest in the baked goods 4H class and became friends, but they were each other's greatest competition, so they were also enemies. Frenemies," she explained.

"Like me and Piedmont," Ethan said.

"No," Piedmont said, shaking his head.

"I'm growing on him," Ethan stage whispered.

"You have that effect on all of us," the woman said, and Blue snickered.

"I love you, Jane," he muttered absently. "Okay, here we go. A week after he filed for divorce, Paley's husband took out a hundred thousand dollar life insurance policy on her. And his girlfriend. And, let's see here, he's in debt up to his eyeballs and somehow managed to purchase a new car with fifty thousand dollars cash."

"Someone got a loan from a shark," Ethan surmised.

"And someone is trying to use the women in his life to pay it off," Blue added.

Piedmont's phone buzzed with a text from an unknown number.

He held it aloft and read out loud, "We have your girlfriend. We want a million in crypto currency in an hour or she's dead."

Blue held out his hand for the phone, and Piedmont handed it over. "Let's see where this came from," he muttered and started to type again. "Here we go, not too far away, at a warehouse downtown." Piedmont reached for his phone, but Blue shook his head. "I need to set up a dummy account, fake the money transfer, buy Ethan some time to get in and out."

"You can do that?" Piedmont said, impressed.

"I can do anything," Blue said, smiling. "Now you two better scoot."

"Thank you," Piedmont said. "I owe you so much."

"Yes, you do," Blue agreed. "Make a generous donation to the Egyptian anthropology collection at the Smithsonian, and we'll call it even."

"Okay," Piedmont said, not understanding but willing to comply.

"Good luck," Jane called, "and thank you for your donation."

"I didn't understand any of what happened in there," Piedmont said once he and Ethan were out of the apartment.

"Blue's a hacker, Jane's an anthropologist at the Smithsonian," Ethan said.

"Oh," Piedmont said. "Who's Becket?"

"No one, it's nothing," Ethan said tightly.

Piedmont barely listened, instead realigning the previous encounter through the new filter. At the moment, he had a hard time thinking of anything at all. His entire mind and body hummed, so tightly strung he would probably twang if bumped. He vibrated with nervousness and anxiety. All the what ifs of the situation ran through his brain with lightning speed.

In contrast, Ethan was perfectly relaxed, his perpetual half smile on his face. As he'd said, this wasn't his first time. "What am I doing?" Ethan said suddenly, stopping short.

"Rescuing Paley," Piedmont reminded him.

"No, I mean why are you with me? Stay here with Blue and Jane. I'll come back for you when it's over."

"No."

"No?" Ethan said.

"No. I'm not staying behind again. I'm going with you this time," Piedmont decreed. He expected an argument, but Ethan shrugged one shoulder and resumed his smile.

"Suit yourself, here we go." They loaded into the car and took off.

CHAPTER 25

"Traffic's going to be tight, and we'll have some time in the car. Tell me about Paley," Ethan commanded.

Piedmont blew out a breath he didn't know he'd been holding. He turned to stare out the window at the gathering darkness and sea of taillights. DC traffic was at its worst, increasing his anxiety. What if they got there too late? What if… "Paley's the best friend I've ever had. She's helped me realize things about myself I didn't know existed, components of my makeup I didn't realize were missing and important. She taught me what it means to be normal and how to accomplish it. She's kind to me in ways I didn't know I needed her to be. She gets me, doesn't try to change me, makes me better, makes me laugh, takes care of me, lets me take care of her."

"That's heartwarming, Bonvoy, but I meant does she keep a cool head in emergencies? Will she take direction if I give her an order? Should I expect someone hysterical and obstinate, what?" Ethan said.

"Oh," Piedmont said, glad for the cover of darkness that hid his flush. "She'll keep a cool head, and she'll listen if she realizes you're one of the good guys."

Ethan nodded. "Sounds like you love her in a forever kind of way."

Was it possible there was a tinge of remorse in his tone, as if he actually felt bad about his part in breaking Piedmont's heart? Would Piedmont feel bad, if the situation were reversed? It was hard for him to imagine now. Every time he tried to imagine stealing Amelia away from Ethan his mind instead conjured Paley. He certainly hadn't felt regret when he thought he was taking Paley away from Mattie. On the contrary, he had felt a vindicated sort of possession, an unwavering certainty that Paley belonged to him and not Mattie, regardless of their long friendship. Was that what Ethan had felt for Amelia? Until this moment Piedmont assumed Ethan was merely the sort of man who took what he wanted, regardless of the consequences. But maybe not. Maybe he only took what he felt already belonged to him.

"Yes," he said in answer to the question that had been asked a while ago, leaving awkward silence too long in its wake.

"Knowing your taste in women, she must be something special," Ethan said.

"She is," Piedmont agreed. He thought of Paley, who had watched her best friend die in the worst sort of way, and yet hadn't given in to despair or given up on life. She had been cheated on and dumped by her husband, ruthlessly kicked to the curb and humiliated by his behavior, but hadn't become bitter or given up on love. She remained unerringly kind and softhearted, humble, hard working, funny, and smart. She was everything he didn't know he needed and wanted in a woman, and she had fallen into his life as if by some miracle. Or perhaps not. Acacia who, besides Paley and his mother, knew him better than anyone, had said she had a feeling about Paley from the beginning, a sort of foreknowledge she and Piedmont would hit it off. She had meant it to be merely a working relationship, but the chemistry that made them work as boss and employee had translated, first into friendship and then romance. Amelia had been glitzy, glamorous, stunningly beautiful and ambitious. For a while, Piedmont believed that was what he needed in life, someone whose accomplishments and status matched his own. But really he needed someone who filled in his missing pieces, who felt like home and peace and love, who provided all the softness he was otherwise missing. Paley liked simple things—sunshine on warm dirt, a cup of tea on a cold afternoon, frosting a cake with precision, reading a good book. Her gentle steadiness had invaded all the missing pieces of Piedmont's heart and life, filling it with warmth and care. How had he never realized how lonely he was? How empty and near to broken? His unusual childhood had given him a bevy of achievements but little else. Now at last he'd found his center, his very heart, and she was in terrible danger.

"Can we not go any faster?" he asked.

"No need, we're here," Ethan said. He parked the car on the street, reached into his bag, and handed Piedmont a vest and helmet.

"I can't take these away from you," Piedmont said.

"You're not. I always bring two in case I have to take Amelia with me when I bug out." He said it normally, as if everyone kept a bag loaded with tactical equipment for his wife, in case he was attacked in the night or some other catastrophe.

"Yes, well, I keep extra socks in my briefcase, so it's practically the same," Piedmont said.

Ethan snickered. "I find you a lot funnier when you're not dating the woman I'm in love with."

"And I find you more likeable when I know you're not going to end up marrying the woman you're rescuing for me," Piedmont returned.

"We'll see how it turns out," Ethan said, then held up his hands. "I was joking, geez. And don't tell Amelia I said that, please. She doesn't take kindly to references of my former player lifestyle."

"Whipped," Piedmont coughed.

"Yeah, we'll see how marriage turns out for you," Ethan said, his tone cryptic.

Piedmont didn't reply because he wasn't married and still rarely won an argument with Paley.

Ethan handed him a gun. "Ready?"

"Yes," Piedmont said, but it came out like a question.

Ethan paused. "Are you having second thoughts? You don't have to do this."

"I'm not having second thoughts; I'm surprised you're letting me do this, frankly," Piedmont said.

Ethan shrugged. "I'm like a dog. The world's all shades of gray to me. If you want to go in and take out a bad guy, that's one less for me to have to handle. I could do this myself, but it seems important for you to want to help, and I sort of owe you. So have at it."

"I don't think I understand your world at all," Piedmont said.

"That's mutual. I'd make a lousy lawyer. I don't see the point of using words when a fist to the face makes a better and more lasting argument." He checked his gun one last time and stepped out of the car, Piedmont at his side. He gave him a rundown of the hand signals he would be using in the raid and then it was, "go time," the last words Ethan whispered before going silent and switching to signals.

Ethan went first, of course. Piedmont didn't fool himself he was anything more than a prop to this SEAL turned spy who could likely kill a man with his bare hands and probably had. Idly, Piedmont wondered how he lived with the death of another man on his conscience but reasoned, despite his words to the contrary, things must be very black and white for him. When wrong was committed, justice must be meted. He was justice's foot soldier. Whereas Piedmont had always been more involved in the ethical deliberations of right and wrong, using logic, reason, and the power of persuasion to come to a conclusion, Ethan saw only two possible outcomes: guilty and in need of punishment or innocent and able to walk free.

They reached a locked door deep inside the warehouse. So far they'd encountered no one, no security. Piedmont wasn't sure if this meant they felt so secure in their hideout they believed they wouldn't be found or they were walking into a trap. He glanced at Ethan to see what he was thinking, but his face was expressionless, his focus on the task at hand complete. It was likely how Piedmont looked when writing a brief or preparing a closing argument. To each his own, he had time to think before Ethan put his ear to the door, listened for a moment, touched his finger questioningly to the hinges, then gave it a hard kick that sent it flying into the room.

Everything happened at once, and the scene turned chaotic. There was a scream, a yelp, and Piedmont froze. As if anticipating this, Ethan used his free hand and drew him into the room while keeping his right hand on his gun, the gun that was now trained on the man in the middle of the room.

Belatedly, Piedmont remembered he also had a gun. He also raised it onto the man, which would have been overkill except the man in question also had his gun raised and trained squarely on Paley's head.

Paley stood beside a single bed, her husband's pregnant girlfriend sprawled on the mattress, weeping. "Shh," Paley said, somewhere between annoyed and soothing.

Piedmont's brain seemed to work slowly and yet on high speed at the same time. He took in the scene and understood it in an instant. His first instinct was to take a shot at the man with the gun. But he might miss. Ethan could take the shot and likely wouldn't miss, but he didn't. He stood still, hand outstretched, gun pointed at the man's head. It occurred to Piedmont that there was a reason Ethan didn't take the shot, and he quickly understood what it was. The person holding the gun was little more than a boy, possibly nineteen at the most. He had a baby face, his hands shook, and he cried.

"You're going to have to lower the gun, or I'm going to kill you," Ethan said slowly and carefully, but the boy cried harder. He could slip and shoot his weapon, harming or killing one of the women by accident. Ethan must have thought the same thing because his hand tightened on his gun.

"You haven't hurt anyone here," Piedmont said, his tone soothing. He lowered his gun. "I'm a lawyer, and I can help you. But that's not going to be possible if you fire that gun."

The boy blinked at him. "You're a lawyer?"

"Yes, and I'm friends with the District Attorney. Put your gun down, and I'll tell him you cooperated. I'll put in a good word on your behalf. But if you don't put the gun down right now, I'll make sure you get the maximum penalty with no leniency."

"He's serious. He's really good, and he'll help you," Paley added. By her tone Piedmont guessed maybe she had already been working on the boy, trying to soften him up and develop a friendship. "He's kind of famous."

The boy blinked at him, sniffling. Slowly, he lowered his gun. Ethan went forward and took it before turning the boy around and securing his wrists with a zip tie. "Where's your partner?"

"He had to get sewn up. She winged him in the arm," he said, nodding toward Paley. Once the boy was secure, Ethan pulled out his phone and made a call, presumably to Cameron who would figure out what to do with the kid. They had the capacity to arrest people, but didn't often do it because of all the bureaucratic lines it crossed.

"Are you okay?" Piedmont said, going forward to grasp Paley's biceps and inspect her.

"Yes," she said, but it came out sounding like a question. "What are you doing here?"

"I..." he began but didn't know how to finish. He had wanted to be the one to rescue her. She looked at him as if he were a hero, as if he had singlehandedly burst into the room and saved her life. But all of a sudden he realized that was how she always looked at him. She didn't need him to physically rescue her from danger; she needed him to love her. And he did. "I have no idea." He gave a little self-deprecating laugh and shook his head. "I'm no good at this stuff. If I were in court, I'd say I had temporary insanity when I heard you'd been taken."

"We might need to dial back the shooting lessons. You've gone full cowboy," Paley said, reaching up to tenderly brush his temple.

"No more, I'm done. And I'm afraid I have some bad news. This little venture has nothing to do with me," he said.

"I know. I figured that out when they took her," she thumbed to the woman on the bed. Piedmont couldn't remember her name, but she cried bitterly. "It was Aaron."

"No, it wasn't," the woman spouted, her tone filled to the brim with angry bitterness.

"She's been a ray of sunshine," Paley said.

"I called an ambulance for her, the cops for him," Ethan interjected.

Paley jumped as if noticing his presence for the first time. "Ethan, what are you doing here?"

"How do you know Ethan?" Piedmont asked.

"There's a picture of him at Amelia's salon," she said with a sheepish half smile.

"You went to Amelia's salon?" Piedmont exclaimed.

"You dated Amelia for months, and you don't recognize her handiwork?" Ethan said, picking up a chunk of Paley's hair. "No one else does highlights like my baby girl."

Piedmont gave him a look. "Right, I'll stop talking and let go of your girlfriend's hair now," Ethan said, taking a step away from Paley.

"I'm not his girlfriend; I'm his housekeeper," Paley said.

"Whatever works for you," Ethan said, then made a zipping motion across his lips when Piedmont gave him another look.

"No, flip that around. I ran into Ashley Benholt at the courthouse this morning. Your divorce is official, Paley Anderson," Piedmont said, giving her biceps a squeeze. Outside sirens wailed, the sound growing louder.

"If I'm going to be your girlfriend, I'm going to need a massive raise," Paley said.

"What? As my housekeeper you said I'm paying you too much, but as my girlfriend you want more?"

"Piedmont, it's so obvious. Girlfriends are way more expensive," she said.

"True story," Ethan said, and this time they both looked at him. "Yeah, I'm not so good at the staying quiet thing."

"I'm seriously beginning to doubt Amelia's choices in life," Paley said.

"I'm finally beginning to understand them," Piedmont said.

"This is so cute. I'm not usually present for the happily ever after part," Ethan said, smiling fondly as his gaze bounced between them. "Except my own. And, again, I'm no expert, but I think now is when you kiss her."

"It could not get more awkward," Paley said.

"Yeah, it could because your husband's mistress's water broke," Ethan said, pointing to the bed.

"Uh-oh," Paley said.

"It's okay, I did a year of med school before law school," Piedmont said. "I was a bit undecided. I know all the technical aspects of delivering a baby, in case the ambulance doesn't arrive."

The pregnant lady screamed.

"Something tells me the feelings are vastly different and not something you want to experience," Paley said. "It's okay, Melinda, he was joking. The squad will be here in minutes, I can hear them outside."

"Shut up," Melinda screamed, gripping the bed. "I hate you."

"I'm going to miss her when this is over," Paley said, and Ethan and Piedmont laughed.

Officers arrived, followed by the ambulance. Melinda was loaded and taken away, still screaming and angry. Paley assured everyone she was fine and didn't need looked over. She gave her statement to the officers, along with a location they could probably find Aaron. As promised, Piedmont called the DA and put in a good word for Paley's captor and a bad one for her husband who had masterminded the whole thing for the insurance money to pay off the loan sharks he owed. By the time he was finished with the call, a warrant had been issued for Aaron's arrest.

At some point after the officers arrived, Ethan slipped out undetected. Piedmont would have to call him later to say thanks, but then again maybe not. In Ethan's mind they were probably even, and in Piedmont's mind, too. Instead maybe he would have Paley help him pick out a combined and belated wedding gift for both Ethan and Amelia.

They sat on the bed, avoiding the wet spot where Melinda's water broke, holding hands, watching activity swirl around them.

"I'm sorry I missed your dinner last night," Paley said.

"You didn't. They rescheduled for next week when you're available," he said.

"I'm still sorry. I hated that we fought, that I hurt your feelings."

"I was being overly sensitive."

"Still, I felt horrible, and I wouldn't have gone if it hadn't been important," Paley said.

"Mattie told me about Jenny."

"Oh."

"Why didn't you tell me?" he asked.

"Because I've spent so much of our relationship in the gutter. I didn't want it to be one more thing about me that needed saving," she said.

"What are you talking about?" he asked.

"Piedmont, when I came to you I had been both fired and dumped. I had no place to live, no money, the world's junkiest car, and an emotionally insulating layer of fat."

"But, Paley, you're the one who got the job, held on to your dignity despite how often your husband tried to take it away from you, and got in shape physically. I had nothing to do with any of that. You're the one who pulled me out of my self-pitying heartache, made me laugh again, taught me what people are talking about when they incessantly reference The Breakfast Club, as well as how to play every conceivable sport," he said.

"Maybe if I'm hearing you correctly, we rescued each other," she suggested.

"While we're being honest, I have to tell you I don't have any idea how things are going to work going forward. Can I actually pay you to keep being my housekeeper if we're together?" he asked.

"No, it's too weird."

"I don't want another housekeeper," he said.

"Do you want to break up already? That must be some kind of record," she said.

"No, I don't want to break up ever."

"How about if I keep doing everything I've already been doing, but this time because I love you and not because you're paying me to do it," she suggested.

"That seems disproportionately unfair to you," he said.

"Why? They're all the things I love to do and without the constraint of being your employee, I can cater more. I've had other offers," she said.

"You have?"

"A few. Not enough to make a fulltime career of it, but enough for some spending money."

"You mean plant money," he said.

"Yes, I'm going to start on the front this week," she said.

The officer in charge of the scene cleared them to go and they walked hand in hand to the car the officers had also summoned, since Paley and Piedmont were without their phones. Charles held the door for them, looking properly dazed and upset over the day's events.

"Piedmont," Paley said when they were safely tucked in the back seat.

"Yes."

"I'm officially divorced," she said.

"You are."

"I told you I love you."

"You did?" he asked, surprised.

"It was in there, if you were listening," she said.

"I totally was," he assured her.

"Okay. I guess we're all caught up," she said, turning to stare out her window.

"You're really tipping my hand here," Piedmont said. Reaching into his pocket, he set a small box on her knee.

She opened it with shaking fingers and pulled out a small, plastic card. "You bought me a lifetime pass to the botanic garden?"

"For inspiration. I actually argued with Mattie about it because he said you'd prefer season tickets to basketball. I don't think he knows about your gardening proclivities."

"It's a relatively new acquisition, and this is definitely so much better than basketball, thank you," she said.

"I had a whole thing planned where I was going to take you out to a nice dinner and grovel for being such a jerk. Then I was going to present you with this and tell you I'm crazy and intensely in love with you and willing to wait, no matter how long your divorce takes. But you kind of wrecked my big, romantic plan by getting kidnapped and interrupting our dinner reservations. Then your divorce got finalized, and it skewered my speech about being willing to wait. But despite all that, I still love you and I'm ridiculously thankful you came into my life."

"That was incredibly sweet and heartfelt," Paley said.

"I sense a 'but' coming on," he said.

"I think you were supposed to follow it with a kiss, and instead we're sitting here awkwardly staring at each other," she said.

"I'm waiting to make my move," he said.

"What are you waiting for?"

"The perfect moment. It's been a long time building. I can't kiss you because it's the expected next step," he said.

"You really can," she assured him.

"No, trust me, it's going to be worth the wait," he said.

"Maybe your perfect moment won't be my perfect moment," she said.

"What's that supposed to mean? Are you saying when I decide to kiss you, you're going to refuse?"

"Maybe."

"Uh-oh."

"What?" she asked.

"My competitive spirit has awoken."

"What does that mean?"

"It means you're going to have to be the one to give in because now I can't," he said.

"It would seem we're at a stalemate here," she said.

"Do I need to remind you I'm undefeated in the courtroom?"

"Are you equating physical affection with winning a case?" she countered.

"You may be onto something there. Let's bookmark that and come back to it in time," he said. "The point is I have an iron will, and I'm going to break you."

"Challenge accepted. Care to seal it with a kiss?"

"It's going to take more than that to break me," he said.

"Let's see how much," she said.

"Challenge accepted."

Two months later, they remained at an impasse, and the strain wore on both of them. They had taken to baiting each other into ending the stalemate, with no success other than to drive the other crazy.

Paley had started wearing her workout gear nearly round the clock, to garden, to cook, to serve breakfast and supper. Piedmont pretended not to notice and paid for it by twice running into walls and once falling off the treadmill.

Piedmont first tried to woo her with gifts—flowers, chocolate, even a bottle of expensive vanilla. Next he turned to physical touch, sliding his fingers gently along her forearm when they sat together on the couch, sifting his fingers through her hair. Mentally, they were ready to snap. Physically, they were hanging tough.

Now Piedmont was about to play his first league baseball game with the other partners. He was nervous and trying not to be.

"You're going to do fine. Your batting is really coming along. You've gotten better in each practice," Paley said.

"Thank you," Piedmont said, a bit snappishly. He should be happy she was fully clothed in shorts and a t-shirt, her hair in a ponytail and topped with a baseball cap, but it was a reminder of the first day he met her and his heart pinged, wanting to reach out, to draw her close, to end the ridiculous standoff once and for all.

Too soon they arrived at the baseball field and were met by Arthur. "It might be a wash; we don't have a pitcher."

"I don't know how strict your rules are, but I could pitch," Paley volunteered.

"Brilliant," Arthur said, leading her forward to present to the umpire.

"Whoa, whoa, whoa." Someone from the opposing team stepped forward. "We're going to trust Piedmont's girlfriend to pitch? No offense, Paley." It was Thomas, the District Attorney and Piedmont's good friend. Paley had also gotten to know him over the last few weeks of discussing Aaron's case, as well as the case of her captor.

"Offense taken, Thomas. I baked you scones. That's like becoming blood brothers in my world," Paley said.

Arthur laughed. "It's either Paley or no game, Thomas."

"Are you scared?" Piedmont taunted.

Thomas put his hands up. "Fine, Paley it is."

"No more scones for you," Paley said, making a slitting motion across her throat. She still held Piedmont's hand and gave it a squeeze. "A kiss for luck?"

"You're diabolical," he whispered, kissing the top of her head before trotting to the dugout.

No one but Piedmont had ever seen Paley pitch before, and therefore no one but him knew how badly she cheated, tossing as many easy lobs to his team as she could get away with and pitching no hitters to the opposing team, all while making it look like she wasn't.

"I'm fairly certain you cheated," Thomas accused when the game was over.

She shrugged. "I've always been an inconsistent pitcher. What can I say? I'm just a girl."

"You're a cheater," Thomas insisted.

"Prove it, counselor," Paley said.

"You owe me double scones," Thomas said, putting her in a headlock.

"Roughing the pitcher, foul, penalty," Piedmont said, removing her from his clutches.

"My hero," Paley said, jumping on his back.

"I've never carried a girl on my back before," he said.

"We'll put it on the list and scratch it off," Paley said. He carried her to the car and held the door for her. "Are you sure you want to go tonight?"

"I'm sure I don't, but it's my first function as a partner, so it's rather vital I attend," he said. "But if you're adamant, I can get us out of it."

"No, I'm good. I bought a new dress."

He groaned. "It's no doubt going to be gorgeous and tempting."

"It's strapless," she agreed, nodding.

"You're killing me," he said.

"I'm trying my best," she said.

Later that night they arrived at the same hall where they attended their first event together. "Déjà vu," Paley said as they stood at the entrance to the room and surveyed the landscape. She now recognized several familiar faces, including Thomas, Arthur, and Brewster. They mingled, saying hello to several of Piedmont's friends and colleagues, and then encountered a new group, someone Paley had never met before. Piedmont tensed, and Paley wondered why until he made the introduction.

"Paley, may I introduce Biffy and Rover Huntington."

Paley blinked twice, trying hard to force her expression to remain neutral, adamantly refusing to glance at Piedmont, lest she lose it completely. Somehow in all the months she'd been attending these events, she had avoided meeting the famed Biffy and Rover. To make matters worse, Biffy had a dog in her purse that kept popping its head out, and Rover insisted on calling Piedmont, "Old Bean." Sensing Paley's veneer was wearing thin, Piedmont made an excuse for them to get away and led her behind the velvet curtain where she bent over laughing. Every time she thought she had herself under control, the laughter started again.

"Her dog was cross eyed," she said, breathlessly, bending over and clutching her stomach again. Finally, at long last, she stood up and sucked oxygen, tamping down the giggles. "How's my mascara?"

"Not good," Piedmont said. He cupped her face, wiping the smudges away, and then he kissed her. She responded, standing on her toes with a sound between a sigh and a whimper.

"Really," she said when the kiss was over. "I've thrown myself at you in multiple different ways, and hysterical laughter was what pushed you over the edge?"

"No, it was the memory of our first time behind this curtain. When I touched your face all those months ago, that was when I realized I was in love with you."

"My realization came later that night, when you bowled a 47 in a tuxedo," she said.

"Weird," he said.

"Weird is my calling card," she said.

"I know, and I love it." He reached for her again when someone pushed aside the curtain to reveal them.

"I wondered whose disembodied feet these were," Thomas said. "I should have guessed."

"Sorry," Paley said, her cheeks going immediately pink.

"It's okay, we've all taken a turn behind the curtain," Thomas said.

"Hopefully not with Piedmont," Paley said, and Thomas laughed.

"I was actually looking for you because your ex hashed out his plea agreement today. He'll serve twelve months."

"Great, thanks," she said. "Why don't you come over for brunch on Sunday? Bring a date."

"Will there be scones?" Thomas asked.

"Two kinds," Paley promised.

"I'll be there," Thomas said. "Carry on, young ones." He closed the curtain and disappeared.

"I think you fit better in this world than I do," Piedmont noted. "A good thing since you're going to be in it for the rest of our lives."

"Are you proposing to me behind a curtain?" she asked.

"Do you see a ring? That was merely a statement of fact," he said.

"Although it's kind of cozy back here. What are the odds we could get away with hiding back here for the remainder of this event?"

"That'll be our thing for the night, to see how long we can last behind the curtain before being rediscovered," Paley said. "Although we should think up a good excuse for why we're back here, in case it's someone important."

"I love how you don't think the DA is important," Piedmont said.

"It's hard to think of him that way when I've seen his face covered in scone crumbs," Paley said. "I meant a judge, and none of this local nonsense."

"Federal?" he suggested.

"Higher," she said.

"Are you trying to tell me we have to remain behind this curtain unless discovered by a member of the Supreme Court?" he asked.

"Yes, and don't say it's impossible because I saw two of them out there," she said.

"Still, the odds aren't great. We could be here a while."

"If only we had some way to fill the time," Paley said. "I wish I knew someone really smart to think of a solution, a genius perhaps."

"This is your lucky night in so many ways," Piedmont said, reaching for her again.

Thank you for reading The Baker and the Barrister, the fifth book in the Spies Like Us series. If you enjoyed this book, please check out my website, www.vanessagraybartal.com for more books.

ABOUT THE AUTHOR

Vanessa Gray Bartal is a foodie who spends her time trolling bakeries and dreaming of new ways to use sourdough. When she is not baking (or eating), she loves to make music and spend time with her husband, three children, and sheepadoodle in rural Ohio. Her dream is to fill her books with enough coziness and warmth to brighten someone's day and make them smile. She would love to hear from you on Facebook or through email.

www.ingramcontent.com/pod-product-compliance
Lightning Source LLC
Chambersburg PA
CBHW031247210726
48287CB00003B/931